PRINCE OF SAND

Frost Book 2

ARIA NOBLE

STERLING & STONE

PRINCE OF SAND

Chapter One

FOUR DAYS.

Ember had never felt so trapped. Not in Dusk, where being inside at least meant a scrap of safety and warmth. Not in Frost, where the walls hemmed her in from all sides but at least there were interesting things to see and do inside them.

Four days.

She marked time with the arrival of night, so it was perhaps more accurate to think that she'd been in this room for four nights.

Which was, really, almost five days.

It was a nice enough room. Warmer than anywhere she'd ever been and containing a rather comfortable chair and even a small, soft mat to sleep on. The walls were made of some kind of thick mud-like substance, lumpy and pale orange like the sand that stretched toward every horizon, and there was a small window cut out of one wall that offered her a view of the little square outside of the building. She was brought food and water three times a day by a silent person covered from head to toe in black cloth so that not even their eyes were visible from beneath it.

She wasn't, so far as she could tell, being treated unkindly.

But the door was locked, and the person with the food never made a single sound, even when Ember tried to get them to answer her. She didn't even know if the person was a man or a woman, only that it wasn't the same person who'd brought her to this room, told her to stay put until the prince called for her, and locked the door tight.

Ember wasn't used to locked doors. Even Frost, with all its walls and secrets, didn't bother locking most of its doors.

And now, she'd nearly worn a hole in the floor with all her pacing.

She worried about Felix and Eli, who she hadn't seen or heard since being locked inside this room. Four days might be long enough for Eli to have sickened and died from the stab wound he'd had in his side from the queen of Frost's Envoy. The wound itself hadn't been especially fatal, made to make a point rather than try to kill, but it needed attention. Attention Ember herself wasn't much able to give it, yes, but at least she knew about keeping wounds clean and wrapped.

What about out here in the desert? What did they do for wounds? Was someone looking after Eli? Keeping his wound clean and dry and bandaged?

Four days was a long, long time. Long enough for even a strong, healthy man like Eli to sicken if not properly looked after.

And, in the moments where she wasn't worrying about Eli, she was worrying about Felix. He hadn't been injured in the fight to get out of Frost, but he was out of Frost for the first time in his life. His queen had been nearly a goddess to him, and here he was now, with inarguable, inescapable proof that she'd lied to and manipulated him and everyone he'd ever known.

There was a world south of Frost, and not only that, it was a habitable world with people in it. Towns. Houses and buildings and squares — different from Frost, but not necessarily lesser.

Ember had seen flashes of fear and doubt in Felix before, and she could imagine how terrible they felt. And now? What was he feeling now? And who was helping him to cope with those feelings?

She could only speculate, and imagine, and worry. And none of those were helping anyone do anything.

Four days.

She paced the room. She ate her meals without even really tasting them. She drained the water — the heat made her thirsty in a way that felt like she would never be sated again. She worried. And, when it all became too much, she collapsed into the comfortable chair and fiddled with her compass.

It was the riddle of the compass, perhaps, that kept Ember from going completely mad. One of the few trinkets that survived from Before, it had been manufactured when things like it were manufactured, and her father had treasured it. When he disappeared, Ember had taken to treasuring it in his stead. She'd brought it from Dusk to Frost, then made sure to take it from the copter when the cloth-covered man came to fetch them from it four days ago. She hadn't been searched before coming into this room, but even if she had, she wouldn't have let anyone take the compass from her.

A few days before setting out for Frost, the compass had suddenly gone from always indicating north the way a compass ought, to pointing south — actually, slightly southwest, rather than properly due south the way it used to point due north. She'd been looking over it, trying to figure out what had happened, ever since.

Now, the compass was doing all kinds of weird things. Sometimes it pointed southwest like it had been this whole time, but sometimes it spun around as if unsure of where it was even supposed to point, and despite the amount of time and effort she spent trying to figure out what was happening, Ember hadn't cracked it.

It kept her relatively sane inside the locked room to have something to puzzle over, but the puzzle itself was starting to drive her almost as mad as the locked door and the worry about her friends.

Ember wasn't used to not understanding what she was looking at, and she didn't like it.

A KNOCK on the door startled Ember out of her frustrated staring at the compass. It was doing that spinning again, the needle swinging around the face of the compass even though the whole thing was sitting still on the low table Ember had pulled around to the front of the chair as a sort of workspace.

But it wasn't just the noise that startled her — it was equally the fact that there'd been a knock on the door. People in Sand, at least as much as she'd learned of them, didn't knock.

"Uh. Come in," she called when she realized that the knocker was waiting for the invitation.

The lock clicked, and a person draped all over with cloth stepped into the room. Though Ember couldn't see anything about their features, she knew that this was a different person than had brought her meals for the last several days — this new person was noticeably taller than

4

the last, and lacked the weary hunch to their shoulders and spine than the previous one — maybe multiple ones — had. Ember straightened in their presence almost without thinking, surprised that a person so swathed in clothing that she wondered how they were able to see could make her feel embarrassed for how poor her own posture was.

The person didn't speak, only gestured silently with one cloth-covered hand for Ember to follow.

Ember stood and followed the person out of the room, though not without some trepidation. It felt good to stretch her legs, but the strange silence of these invisible people always put her on edge.

"Where are we going?" she asked, her voice barely more than a whisper. It didn't even echo in the thick-walled hallway they'd stepped into.

The person shook their head and waved again for her to follow.

"You're not the same one as last time, are you?"

Another shake of the head.

A spark of hope lit up Ember's thoughts. The other — others? — had never even done that much, never even would move their heads in answer to Ember's questions.

Maybe this one was different. Willing, in their own silent way, to communicate with her.

"My friends. Are they okay?"

The person didn't answer.

"I came here with two others. Boys. One of them about this tall, a little older, dark hair and skin like me, a wound on his side. The other one with fire-red curls, you couldn't miss him. Have you seen them? Are they okay?"

The person just kept walking.

"Please. Just ... have you seen them?" Ember fought to keep the sob out of her voice. "Heard about them? Anything?"

Finally, slowly, the person shook their head again.

Well. It wasn't much of an answer, certainly not one she wanted, but she couldn't hope for this person to tell her Eli and Felix were okay if they didn't even know who they were. She beat the thoughts down.

This person didn't know them. Hadn't seen them. Knew nothing about them. It wasn't their fault if they couldn't tell her whether they were all right, or even still alive.

Ember squeezed her eyes shut for a moment, forcing back the sensation of tears before they could fall. At least now she was out of the room, beyond that locked door. Perhaps she could run.

But where would she go? She didn't know where she was, not really. Not well enough to determine where she had to go to get back to anywhere familiar.

And even if she did, even if she knew precisely where she was and was intimately familiar with how to return, where would she return *to*? Dusk? No. There was nothing for her in that dying little village out in the tundra. Frost? She'd run from that city, determined to get to some mysterious place she kept hearing about called Sand. The prince of Sand, whoever that was, had been calling to her.

She thought she was in Sand now. She had no way of confirming that suspicion, but given how she'd been taken here, that seemed the most likely option. Before she left, she would have to find the prince. Figure out what he wanted of her, why he'd been calling to her.

And she would have to find Eli and Felix. They were all in this together, whatever this was. She wasn't going to leave them behind for anything.

For now, though, she figured that keeping her head down and paying attention was the only thing she could reasonably do. That had served her well in the past, and maybe she'd learn something along the way.

The hallway opened up into a sort of courtyard, walled on all sides by more building and roofed with the same sort of light cloth most of the people she'd seen in the area wear. People mingled in clumps around open braziers and scattered kegs, and Ember noticed with a shock that many of those people were smiling the wide, blank smiles of Frost dolls.

In fact, the more she looked at the people, the more dolls she noticed scattered through the crowd. She'd seen dolls before in numbers, of course — sometimes fully half of any Frost crowd could be made up of the empty eyes and unnaturally wide smiles of dolls — but here, it seemed that dolls outnumbered people maybe three to one.

Were they all Frost dolls? Had they crawled through the broken wall like that one trolley driver had?

And, most of all, *why*?

The person Ember followed made a small noise in the back of their throat, low enough to not be heard over the hum of chatter but enough to catch Ember's attention and bring it back to whatever their task was. Ember tucked her questions about the dolls away for a better time and continued to follow the person.

They crossed the courtyard and went into the building again, picking up a hallway as if they'd never left it until it spit them out into a small antechamber. Someone was already sitting in one of the chairs that dotted the space, and Ember's heart leaped with recognition.

Felix.

He jumped to his feet when she came in, and Ember shoved past her guide and ran to him, nearly knocking him back into the chair with the force of her hug.

"Thank the Mother!" she hissed under her breath and

squeezed him tight, trying to reassure herself that he was here and well and whole. Her breath hitched with tearless sobs.

Felix squeezed her back and pressed his face into her shoulder.

They stood like that for a long moment, just holding on tight and grateful to find each other, until slowly Ember pulled back so she could take a closer look at him.

"Hey," he said with a smile when their eyes met.

Ember laughed, and even her laugh sounded like a sob. She scanned him up and down, looking for anything that seemed out of place. Nothing jumped out to her — his clothes, still the Frost style, were pristine, his limbs all appeared to be in their right place, and his smile was warm and normal and perfect. "Are you okay?"

"I'm fine. You?"

"Better now." She looked around the room. If Felix was here, perhaps Eli would be, too.

But there was no one else in the room — even the person all wrapped in cloth had slipped out, leaving them alone.

"He's okay," Felix answered as if reading her thoughts — she probably wasn't being very subtle about them. "The Brothers are looking after him."

"You've seen Eli?"

Felix nodded. "He's getting the medicine he needs."

Ember let out a breath, and it felt like the first full breath she'd had since being locked up in that room. Felix was here, and Eli was okay. She would prefer it if Eli was in the room, too, of course, but she'd take this if it was all she could get. It was more than she'd had in almost five whole days.

She pulled Felix back in for a gentler hug, closed her eyes, and let herself breathe. He smelled clean and warm, a little dusty, but very much like himself. She hadn't realized how much she needed that reassurance until she had it, didn't realize how much she missed his smell until it was there again.

"I'm sorry." He spoke softly, and almost directly into her ear, his breath warm on her skin. "I tried to … but I wasn't allowed in the woman's wing. We've been so worried."

"You've seen Eli. Where is he?"

"Not here in this building. He's in the 'akhelum with the Brothers. He's fine. Healing."

There was something underneath those last couple of words, something that prickled at Ember's attention, but that she couldn't quite grasp. Something more, a significance that she didn't know.

But before she could ask him about it, someone else stepped into the room.

It was a man, not quite as completely swathed in fabric as the people who had served Ember her meals, but still wrapped up from neck to ankle in cloth. Ember pulled away from Felix. Not far — if anyone thought she was going to let go of him any time soon, they were about to be sorely disappointed — but enough that she could face the other man. He was familiar, and that as much as anything struck her as strange. She hadn't seen a face except the ones she'd glimpsed out the window of her room in nearly five days, but she knew this one.

The man scowled. "Can I help you?"

Ember scowled right back. This was the man who'd taken them from the copter. Who had locked her up in that room, split her up from her friends. She would've been perfectly happy to never see his face again. "I don't know. You're the one who brought us here."

The man blinked, once, twice, as if startled by that

response, then his expression cleared with sudden recognition. "Oh! Oh, of course. I'll fetch him right away."

He turned back the way he came.

Ember frowned at Felix but found him frowning just the same, his expression mirroring her confusion perfectly.

This, apparently, was not something Felix already knew.

The man was back in a minute, and someone else, another man, came with him. The new man was dressed in the same sort of style as the first, in a high-necked tunic that stretched all the way to his ankles, but unlike the others Ember had seen in Sand until now, his tunic was colored a deep, rare-sky blue and embroidered all over with golden thread. The wrap around his head was a brighter red even than Felix's hair and undeniably costly and soft.

The prince, Ember guessed, because no one but a ruler would be able to afford such things, surely.

And then she blinked and looked at him again, focusing now on his face rather than the obvious expense of his clothes. Because there was something familiar about him — the shape of his nose and color of his eyes reminded her of nights snuggled around the fire, her child fingers touching words written in bleeding ink and a voice near her ear telling her tales of Before.

Ember took a step toward the man, barely aware of the movement. "Papa?"

Chapter Two

A THOUSAND THOUGHTS flooded her mind. How could this man, the mysterious prince of Sand, be her father? Her father was supposed to have died out in the tundra beyond Dusk when she was seven. Even if he hadn't, even if he'd survived, how could he make it here? The only way she had was by breaking down Frost's southern wall — there was no way he'd done that, too, inside the space of the last decade. Frost would've remembered that. The queen would've remembered that.

But the queen had known Ember's father, or had at least pretended to in order to sweeten the deal for Ember's help, and how much of the queen of Frost's words could Ember really trust? She dealt in lies and corruption, maintained her power by pretending she was capable of much, much more than she really was and threatened her people with the nothingness she claimed was the end of the world if anyone got near the wall.

That much was untrue — Ember had assumed these last five days, and probably much more than that, that everything the queen said was untrue, including what she claimed to know about her father.

Ember bit down on the inside of her cheek, hard enough to hurt, hard enough to distract herself from the whirling inside her own head. Her vision was blurry with tears, a few spilling over her lashes and running hot and fast down her face. She took another step forward, a little more deliberately this time. Her voice cracked. "Papa!"

He didn't look at her. His whole attention was fixed on Felix. He smiled wide, and now there was no question in her mind — she knew that smile, clung to it fiercely for the last ten years, unwilling to forget.

"Well, hello," he said to Felix. "I didn't expect to see you."

Ember sensed Felix's frown, the quick look he shot toward her, as surprised by this greeting as she was by her father's arrival, but she didn't look back at him to confirm that sense. She couldn't take her eyes from her father's face.

Why wouldn't he look at her? Did he not recognize her as she did him?

Perhaps — she'd changed much more in the last ten years than he had.

"Papa. It's me. It's Ember."

She reached out to touch his arm, to pull his attention toward her, but he swatted her hand away, still without looking at her.

She jerked back, more startled than hurt by the strike. Her father had never hit her before, never! A couple more tears, this time confused, slipped over her lashes. She wiped them away unhappily.

"Hey," Felix said, disapproval in his voice. "What're you doing?"

Papa lifted Felix's chin with one hand and tilted his

head this way and that like a customer examining a merchant's wares. He clucked his tongue and grinned. "Excellent. Truly excellent, isn't he, Shahif?"

"Excellent, our royal prince," the other man echoed with a nod.

Felix pulled away from his hand. "Do I know you?"

Papa laughed. "Most excellent!"

Felix looked at Ember, and this time, she looked back.

Why wouldn't he notice her? What was he going on about, speaking about Felix like someone might comment on mittens?

"You're Ember's father?"

At least Felix was trying.

"Mikail Dominikovich. Or 'our royal prince,' if you prefer — I respond to either."

"Uh ... Felix Dmitrivich."

Papa chuckled. "Most excellent. I'm pleased you're here, Felix. We shall have to speak later. Shahif, would you kindly show our guest back to his room?"

The other man bowed, then gestured for Felix to follow him out of the room.

Papa watched them go, waited until the door closed behind them, then at last turned to face Ember. He smiled warmly, his voice going soft. "Ember."

"Papa," she answered.

He opened up his arms, and Ember raced into them.

His tunic was smooth and cooling against her hot face where she buried it into his shoulder, and she fought to keep in the tears lest they stain the pretty blue color, but a few leaked out anyway. "I thought you'd forgotten me."

"Never. I just couldn't have you making a scene in front of my man. You understand."

She did, sort of. If she'd had room for it, she would've been embarrassed by her outburst already — she probably would be embarrassed by it once useful thoughts came back to her. It was probably best for both of them that he'd kept her back until now.

"You got my message. I knew you would, clever girl."

She wasn't ready to think about that — she was still too staggered by the fact that he was *alive* and *here* and *holding her* to have any room for anything else. The possibility that he was sending her messages was something she wasn't ready to handle.

They stood there in silence for a while, Ember clinging to his tunic and Papa rubbing little circles along her spine, and she felt like a child needing to be soothed after a nightmare, but she didn't care.

For ten years, she'd been sure that Papa was gone, that he'd stepped into the tundra beyond Dusk and frozen to death before he had any chance of getting anywhere. For ten years, she'd been sure that she was an orphan, a girl alone in the world with no one but herself and a friend to look after her. She'd come to grips with that idea of herself a long time ago.

And now, to find out that wasn't true, that her father hadn't died somewhere in the featureless expanse of tundra, that he was, in fact, alive and doing well, the prince of a desert town — it was a lot to take in all at once, and Ember wasn't sure what it all meant, where it was supposed to fit in with her understanding of herself and the world around her.

She pushed all that aside. She'd worry about it later, when Papa wasn't holding her.

"There now," he said at last, pulling away. "You're all grown up."

Ember wiped the tears out of her eyes before he could see them and think her childish for them.

"And you've been to Frost."

She nodded. "The queen said there was nothing out here."

His eyebrows went up at that. "You saw Natalya?"

Ember had never heard anyone give the queen a name. And, yes, the queen had referenced knowing Ember's father once or twice, even dropping hints that she knew what had happened to him, but Ember had always assumed those were lies, since everything else the queen said was a lie. "You know the queen of Frost?"

"It's a long story, and now's not the time for it."

Maybe not. Ember was still reeling too hard at her father even being alive. "Have you been here all this time?"

Papa smiled and gestured for Ember to sit in one of the chairs in the room. She did, and he took another, pulling it around so they were facing each other. "We'll talk details some other time. For now, the most important thing is that you're here, and I hope you can help me. You've heard stories of the Leshii?"

Ember frowned. The word sounded a little bit familiar, like something she had heard before, but that escaped her full grasp.

"Perhaps you know it as the Engine."

"Oh!" It came to her then, in a rush. "You mean the great Engine from Before."

"That's the one. Its name is the Leshii, and it lives somewhere out beyond the desert. They called it Forest for its great towering trees and abundance of life, and the Leshii is said to still be there, waiting for the person who can fix it, repair its broken pieces and restart its inner workings."

Fix the Leshii.

It was a phrase Ember had heard before, but she couldn't quite pinpoint where or why. The words just hovered there, at the edges of her mind, prickling her with their familiarity but refusing to be looked at, like that cluster of stars in the winter sky that were best seen from the corner of the eye and that vanished when looked at straight on. A dream that quickly faded no matter how much her waking thoughts wanted to hold onto it.

Something shifted inside her. It was that little place deep down that had always felt something she didn't know how to describe or explain. Something tugged at that place, as thin and fragile as a single hair, easy to ignore but always, inescapably *there*.

Fix the Leshii.

"The cult here has a prophecy about the person who is to find the engine and restart it," Papa continued, pulling Ember's attention back to him and sending that ghostly phrase and its tiny tugging into the aether where it came from. "It's nonsense, of course, just a jumble of mystical-sounding words that could apply to any number of people and things as all prophecies are, but they've always insisted that I can't be the man of their prophecy. Something about not coming from the clouds." He smiled wanly, making it clear exactly what he thought about any of that, then his face turned serious again, and his eyes fixed on Ember with an intensity that made her swallow against another bout of tears. "You, though. You came in a copter, yes?"

"Yeah. Your man took us out of the copter I rebuilt."

"Rebuilt?"

"It was broken." She sounded like she was bragging and found that she didn't care. She wanted him to know, to think well of her. To tell him that she'd done everything she could to follow in his scientist footsteps, even when he wasn't there to guide her like he had when she was small. "I fixed it."

Papa nodded slowly, thoughtfully, his lips pressed tight together. Ember could see his thoughts turning and wished she knew what they were, what they meant, how she could help them.

"It wasn't very broken," she added after a moment, because she also didn't want to come off as pompous, and the longer those words hung in the silence between them, the more ridiculous they sounded. "And Felix helped me."

"Ah, Felix. How did you two meet?"

Ember fought back a frown. It struck her as odd once again the way he seemed to know the random Frost boy who'd become her friend. "It's not really exciting. He offered me an apple. Well," she added when she felt herself blushing at the memory, "he came up behind me, and I would've put a knife in his gut for startling me, except I forgot my knife. Then he offered me an apple."

Papa laughed, and it was just as Ember remembered it — a full, deep sound that creased his eyes and flashed his teeth. "You're a Dusk girl through and through."

Ember flushed harder, unsure if that was meant to be a compliment or an insult.

It was Papa, and he was laughing. Of course it was meant to be a compliment. She felt stupid for even wondering and grateful that she hadn't done her wondering aloud.

He sobered after a moment, though the laugh still sparkled in his eyes. "You're a scientist, then?"

"Not a scientist. But I like to tinker, and I'm pretty good at knowing what's broken and why." She decided not to mention the compass currently sitting in her room that she couldn't fix.

Papa stood and gestured for her to do the same. "Come. I want you to look at something."

He took her out through a different door than she'd come in, into a smaller room dominated by a large mechanical contraption and containing very little else.

Ember scanned the thing automatically, searching for a clue to the machine's purpose and workings. It was meant to be electrical — wires crisscrossed the gears and belts in a mass that wasn't organized but still made a sort of sense: this wire went from this end to that gear, that wire was supposed to carry power from that gear to this piston.

It didn't have any electricity running through it, though, and the whole machine sat still and silent.

She couldn't decide what it was meant to do. There were no blades or vents, no legs or fingers, no obvious work the machine was built for.

"I can't figure it," Papa said. "Everything seems to be in the right place, but when I try to turn it on, nothing happens."

Ember walked around the room, around the machine, searching, letting her attention snag on what it would, waiting for the problem to reveal itself.

It looked a little like Frost's machines, the ones the queen kept insisting were broken but that never appeared to have anything wrong with them. But the queen wasn't mechanical like Papa — if he said this machine wasn't working when he tried, then something had to be wrong.

Maybe this machine was like Frost's. Maybe it was built to keep things cold. Working together, a whole room of machines wasn't capable of holding back the warmth from the other side of the southern wall.

But then, Papa would have the sense to not try to keep a giant wall of ice frozen in the heat of Sand. Whatever he kept cold would be something small and reasonable. Food, maybe — some of the fruits from dinner had been cool even sitting out in the warmth of the qasun.

This machine needed power. Power that it clearly wasn't getting from the upper part where, she thought, the power was meant to be generated.

Ember crouched down, searching the underside. If power wasn't being made the way it needed, perhaps there was a way to rewire it. "What about external power?" she asked, her eyes still tracing along the routes of the wiring. "Is there something you can plug this machine into?"'

Papa padded around to her side, crouched down next to her. "It's not meant for external power. The top is where the electricity comes from."

So she was right about that. Ember fought down a grin — it would hardly do to be smug. "Well, sure. But if you need for the machine to run right now…"

"External power," he repeated. He sounded almost proud. "A battery."

"I think it needs more power. It's just not generating enough to get it started, to overcome the inertia of being turned off." She found what she was looking for then, the set of wires that were used to pull electricity from the top of the machine down to the bottom, where she had at last found the vent the whole thing was meant to run. It was quite a lot like Frost's machines, in fact; the only real difference was that those machines had entirely other, much larger, machines to generate the electricity they needed to run.

Ember squirmed under the machine so she could reach the wires. "These right here? These are your starters. If you had some kind of — yeah, some kind of battery to help it get over that initial hurdle of actually starting, then this machine should be able to produce enough power on its own to keep going."

She wiggled out from underneath the metal and smiled at Papa. "Starting is the hardest part."

He was staring at her, that same thoughtful frown from before tugging at his expression. She felt commanded to hold still as though for an inspection, and she did, but her fingers twitched in the silence.

She hadn't expected him to test her. She could only hope she'd passed.

After a long moment, he put his elbows on his knees and leaned toward her. His voice dropped to a conspiratorial whisper. "We need to find the Leshii, but the only way to do that is to get to the place that will take us there. But that spot, the Spindle, lives behind the Brothers' walls, inside the 'akhelum, and they won't let me near the place. But you…" He smiled then, broad and excited. "You came from the sky like I didn't have the chance to do. If you can convince the Brothers that you're the person their prophecy speaks of, we'll be able to find the Leshii and finally fix the world."

Chapter Three

EMBER FOLLOWED THE OTHER MAN, Shahif, through the qasun. She still wasn't exactly sure what she was supposed to be doing, but figured she'd sort it out once she knew what she was up against.

Shahif paused at one of the doors, and Ember guessed that was the door outside. She remembered, vaguely, that most of what she thought of as Sand existed inside the walls of this building, that beyond it was little more than the desert she and the boys had flown over for hours after breaking through Frost's southern wall.

He opened the door and bowed to her from the waist. "Mustafi," he mumbled, as if he expected that word to have any meaning to her.

It didn't, but he said it with such feeling that she didn't feel like she was allowed to question it.

"Move quickly," he added as she stepped from the shelter of the walls into the blazing heat of the desert. "Don't let the monsters see you."

Ember bit her lip to keep down her worry about

monsters. Because they were certainly unfounded, a fear based on another of the lies the queen told her people about the world beyond the wall.

Here, there be dragons.

But none of it was real, so she wouldn't let herself be afraid of a lie.

Beyond the qasun walls, there was, as she'd remembered, very little. Sand and sun stretched from horizon to horizon, and while Ember, as someone who had grown up in the cold and dark of Dusk, usually basked in whatever sunlight she could get, she felt almost attacked by it here. The air, the sun, the wind, were as scorching as the tundra was cold, as strange and painful as she remembered it from the hours of flying through it in the copter.

Though she wasn't going to be afraid of stories about unreal monsters, the air and sun and stinging bits of sand encouraged her to move quickly anyway. The 'akhelum, the building she was aiming for, was a few minutes away from the qasun door, and she hurried toward it, eager to get out of the sun as quickly as possible.

Like the qasun, the 'akhelum was a thick-walled building of sand-colored brick, featureless except for the door set into one side. Ember tried the latch, but it wouldn't move.

Lightning crackled on the horizon, and the wind was picking up, sending bits of hair and sand into Ember's eyes. She brushed them clear and squinted against the pain of it.

She knocked and waited.

There was no answer.

But there had to be people inside. The Brothers, who she took to be the cult Papa had mentioned, had taken Eli in to heal him, and Felix had been in and out of the building to see him, so surely someone had to be minding the door at least sometimes.

Ember knocked, harder and longer this time, insisting.

A tiny window on the door slid open, and one dark eye peered out at her. A voice, gravelly, rough, and deeply unfriendly, spoke in a language Ember didn't understand. Though she could tell the words were meant to be some kind of question, she didn't know what it was or how to best answer it.

Ember tried to smile. It wasn't a particularly genuine expression, but it was the closest she could get, and maybe it would fool someone without a good view of her, anyway.

The voice sighed and switched to her own tongue. The words came out with a strange, heavy accent, almost liquid in its speed and lack of distinct sounds. "Who are you?"

"I'm looking for the Spindle."

Those were the words Papa had used to explain to her what she was supposed to be doing at the 'akhelum — she hoped they meant more to the man behind the door than they did to her.

The eye squinted. "Who are you?"

There was a different intonation to the question this time — less "what's your name?" and more "how do you know things we haven't told you?"

Well, since she was already getting a reaction from this man with words others had used with her... "Mustafi," she said, trying to match the inflections Shahif had used to speak the word.

The little window slid shut, but before Ember had to start knocking again, the whole door opened up, and a man stepped out.

Ember's cheeks went hot, hotter than they already were under the sun. The man was almost completely naked —

only a strip of dark cloth wrapped around his hips preserved even the barest bit of modesty. She stepped back instinctively as he came toward her, closing the door behind him.

He looked her up and down with the sort of appraising eye that Ember might be tempted to slap him for, if she could tolerate the idea of getting close enough to touch him. His hair was long and tangled into knots right into his beard, and there was a smell coming off him like he hadn't bathed for the better part of his adult life and was proud of that fact.

"You can't be the mustafi," he said after a moment. "Who sent you? Was it Mikail?"

He spat Papa's name like it tasted bad.

If these were the Brothers, perhaps it spoke to Papa's credit that he wasn't liked by them.

"No one sent me," Ember lied. She lifted her chin, forced down her embarrassment, and met the man's eyes. "I'm looking for the Spindle. Is it here?"

"Can't tell you."

"So it is here."

The man scowled. "That's not what I said."

"This is the 'akhelum?" She tried not to trip over the word, still trying to act her part with total confidence, but she was pretty sure she'd butchered the word just the same.

He spat at her feet. Ember shifted away from the splatter of gooey wet his spit formed in the sand. She was still wearing the light shoes common in Frost, but she didn't want to even brush her shoes against anything that had been inside this man.

"It's a simple question," she tried again. "Is this the 'akhelum? Just answer me that."

The man pressed back against the door. "You're from the qasun. We don't talk to the qasunfi."

24

"You're a Brother?"

He spat again, aiming once more for her feet, and once again, Ember shifted away from it. He grinned at her flinching. Even his teeth, what she could see of them through the tangled mess of his hair and beard, were dirty. He spoke again in that unfamiliar language, and the unfriendliness of it was so obvious that Ember stifled another flinch.

"You have my friend. I just want to see Eli."

The man shook his head. "We don't talk to the qasunfi. You need to leave."

Ember tried to step around him. If she could just get to the door, she was pretty certain she could get in and find Eli. This building, unlike the qasun, didn't appear especially big.

But the man matched her step with one of his own, putting himself toe-to-toe with Ember. "Go away, qasunfi. The mustafi is not for your eyes."

"I'm the mustafi," she tried. She would have to ask Papa what that word meant, but for now, she spoke it like she was sure of it.

The man laughed. The sound was as harsh as his voice, as dry as the wind. "You are not the mustafi. We have already found him."

Ember blinked and hoped it looked like she was just trying to clear her eyes of the sand-blasted air. That wasn't an unreasonable hope — her eyelids were gritty, her eyeballs dry, her skin shrunk and scorched. The storm brewing on the horizon was approaching, and she could see the man glancing toward the lightning every couple of seconds as if judging its speed, and she sensed that it would be unsafe for either of them to be outside the safety of building walls when it actually came.

And in that moment, before she could quite finish

working out what he was saying, before she could finish putting the thoughts into an order that made proper sense, thunder rolled through the desert. The man stepped back, his hand reaching for the door's latch. "Go away, qasunfi," he said again, but this time, there was an urgent edge to his voice. "You're not welcome here."

Ember didn't want to touch him, but she wasn't about to let him back away without at least answering something. She grabbed his arm and refused to flinch at the grit she could feel scraping against her palm. "It's Eli, isn't it? The mustafi? You have him in there?"

The man shoved her back and glanced toward the sky again. The clouds were a strange color, not the white or gray Ember was familiar with, but a greenish-yellow that was disturbing and unnatural.

The wind died. The air crackled.

Ember backed away, encouraged by the shove, but most of her attention, like the man's, had been drawn to the sky.

"You have only a minute," the man hissed suddenly. "Run."

He slipped through the door. She heard the lock thump shut in the strange silence the wind had left behind. Ember took another step back, torn between insisting the man let her in to at least see Eli and doing as he suggested and running for cover.

And, in that moment of hesitation, the storm struck.

EMBER HAD SEEN STORMS BEFORE. Dusk had them about once a week, where the temperature dropped so that you had to stay inside, huddled under your blankets nearly up against the fireplace if you didn't want to freeze to death, and the wind and snow came so hard that you couldn't see

26

the hand in front of your face. Those storms sometimes went on for days at a time, trapping everyone where they were, and there was inevitably at least one corpse dug out from under the drifts after it was over.

But even after a lifetime of surviving Dusk's weather, Ember was not prepared for a Sand storm.

The wind, which had been stinging and hard in the sunshine, knocked her to her knees when it kicked up again, and the moment it touched her bare skin, the heat and scouring sand that came with it raised blisters like she'd actually set herself aflame. Ember gasped in pain, and the air raced down her throat and into her lungs, and she could feel the blisters forming in her mouth and tongue, too, pain tearing down her throat and into her chest where the fire-hot air touched her airway.

Instinctively, she fell forward and pressed her face to the sand, wrapping her blistered arms around her head in an effort to protect it. A moment ago, it would've hurt, the heat rising from the sun-scorched ground too much, but against the touch of the wind, it was almost a soothing cool. At least breathing against the sand didn't feel like swallowing fire, and her arms offered a little bit of shelter from the wind against her face.

The wind kept at her, tearing at her skin until she was sure it was sloughing off, pulling free of her bones and joining the sand in the whirlwind, but she didn't dare lift her face to check.

Then the wind died, almost as quickly as it had come, replaced by something wet and cool on whatever was left of her arms. She had to get out of the weather, she knew. She had to do as the man had suggested and run. Maybe, if she moved quickly enough, she could make it back to the qasun before the wind started up again.

More drops splattered onto her arms. They stung when

they hit the blisters on her skin, but weren't nearly as painful as the wind had been, so she opened one eye and peeked through the tattered hem of her sleeve.

Her vision filled with red. She opened her mouth to pull in a breath, and her mouth filled with the taste of metal and heat.

The wet wasn't rain as she'd thought — it was blood.

Ember lurched to her feet and staggered blindly forward. Clots formed in her hair and fell with horrible wet sounds off of her. The sand was at once slick and sticky with the gore pouring from the sky, and she couldn't see, couldn't hear, couldn't smell anything but blood. It dripped from her fingers and gushed from the ground like the sand itself was a nest of sliced veins. It trickled in strange muddy creeks that clotted at the edges, and shapes grew from those edges into creatures that lowered faceless heads to the streams and drank from them.

She couldn't breathe — each time she tried, she only choked. When she looked down at her hands, she found they were curled and decaying, skin growing black and sloughing off in sheets, exposing the whiteness of her bones beneath.

She couldn't make her fingers move, couldn't uncurl them from the strange clawed form they'd taken, couldn't straighten her fingers. Couldn't even feel her hands anymore.

Something came at her — a monster had lifted its bloody head and was trotting toward her on footless legs, its mouth open and exposing a dozen rows of impossibly sharp teeth.

Ember screamed. She tried to lift her arms up to shield her face again, but her whole body had gone limp and numb, trapping her inside a decaying cage without any way to move or defend herself.

And then it was gone, and a door closed shut between her and the monster.

Chapter Four

HANDS PRESSED AGAINST HER SHOULDERS, and they should be disrupting the blisters on her skin, but they felt just normal and soothing. Ember's scream echoed back at her from the door, but already her vision was clearing, and the pain of the wind, the stench of the blood, was leaching out of her like it had never been.

"Shh, shh," a voice said from behind her. "It's all right. You're all right."

Ember sucked in a couple of breaths to quiet the scream still clawing at her throat and found that the air was no longer blistering, that the pain that had sprouted in her throat and lungs was gone. She glanced down at her hands — the skin was smooth and intact, her fingers straight and covered in flesh, even though a second before she could've sworn her hands had been decaying and red.

"There were ... monsters..." she gasped. "And the blood—"

"Shh, it's all right," the voice said. The hands on her shoulders moved, smoothing down her back and up again, and the touch helped to pull her back down to reality. "It was a bit of a storm, that's all."

She turned, blinked up at the man, struggled to identify him. Not Papa — Shahif. He looked back at her with a little wrinkle between his eyebrows, a frown pinching down the corners of his lips.

She wiped her cheeks, but all that came off them was the gritty damp of tears.

"That's it," Shahif murmured. He kept his hands on her shoulders. "It's all right. We've all been through it."

"What—?"

He shook his head. "A storm. We've all seen them."

"My hands..."

"It wasn't real. See?" He lifted her hand in front of her face but kept hold of her wrist, keeping the pressure of his fingers against her skin as if to assure her it wasn't blistered and decaying. "All's well."

Her breathing was beginning to steady, and with it the spiraling panic. She blinked at her uninjured, unbloodied hand and could almost believe the sight of it.

"Wiggle your fingers," Shahif said.

She obeyed. They moved as they ought to, under her own deliberate control.

"It wasn't real?"

As if to prove her wrong, thunder rumbled through the ground.

Shahif watched her steadily, and that as much as anything made Ember feel better. He was her father's man, and he wasn't going to lie to her. "The storm's real enough, but what it shows you isn't." His frown relaxed. "What did you see?"

Blood. Monsters. Her own hands, crippled, injured — useless.

It sounded insane, even inside her own head. She

pulled away from him and wiped the sand off her face — apparently, she had at least buried her face in the ground, given how much she was able to knock off. "It felt real."

"They always do. But you're safe in here. The storms — they can't touch us here. The walls protect us."

It sounded like something the people of Frost might say. *The wall protects us. If the wall falls, we all do. Here, there be dragons.*

Ember hadn't believed those words, had always assumed the queen had been lying to her people about everything, determined always to keep them under her own control. She'd assumed the wall was a lie, too, that the queen had maintained it only to keep hold of the minds of her people, that everything she and everyone else had said about that giant southern ice wall was lies fed to them by the queen.

Now, she wondered how true those assumptions were.

The queen had lied about what was — or rather, wasn't — on the other side of that wall, as she'd always insisted that there was literally nothing there. But maybe she hadn't been entirely lying about the protection it provided.

Ember had never felt so grateful for protective walls before.

"It's all right," Shahif said again, dropping her hand and stepping away. "I'll summon your woman, and you can go rest."

He turned and hurried down the hall.

She didn't want to rest. Her whole body buzzed with terror and pain, the energy unreleased now that she wasn't actually fleeing for her life. But her head ached, and she was pretty sure she was one uncareful breath away from doing something, saying something, she might not want to say or do.

She'd failed. Her father had sent her out of the building to get into the 'akhelum, find whatever the Spindle was supposed to be. Not only had she not convinced the man to let her through the door, she'd apparently also gotten herself almost killed by the weather.

A whole life lived surviving the brutal weather of Dusk, and somehow the desert was the thing that was truly dangerous.

Shahif returned after a minute with one of the fully-clothed people. Ember supposed it was the same one who'd served her breakfast and brought her out of her room — there was that same straightness and height to their spine that seemed to mark them as different from many of the other covered people — but how could she be sure? Of this person, of Shahif — of anyone, really?

She missed Eli and Felix. She could be sure of them.

Well. Ember straightened and followed the person when they gestured for her. Until she could find out where they were, get in to see them, she would just have to find a way to be sure of herself.

SHE SPENT a couple of quiet hours in her room, watching out the window at the courtyard bustling with dolls and people. The number of dolls in the building quite astonished her. Frost had been dripping with dolls such that you were almost guaranteed to bump into at least one wherever you went, but as she noticed before, here the dolls outnumbered the flesh-and-blood people by at least double and then half again.

She watched them especially, looking for signs of the doll madness she'd been unable to fix in Frost but seeing nothing. Here in Sand, the dolls seemed happy and normal, without the urge to scream about the wall cracking or driving trolleys into it to make a hole.

As the hours ticked on, Ember felt like the horrors of the storm were less and less real. Though it had felt like the whole world while she was inside of it, now that she was in a familiar-ish place, uninjured and calm, the panic, the visions, became as fleeting and impossible to hold as a dream. A nightmare, to be sure, but no more real than a sleeping figment of her imagination.

We've all been through it, Shahif had said, and that felt like both a truth and perhaps even an honor — a test she had suffered through and passed.

She didn't think Papa had sent her out to the 'akhelum knowing a storm was coming, or that Shahif had led her to the door with the intention of testing her that way, but since she'd been out there, caught it, perhaps that meant she was one of them anyway.

At least she knew now to never be outside when the clouds turned that greenish-yellow and lightning tore through the sky.

After a while, the person came back to her room, though they weren't carrying a meal with them. Ember stood, determined to at least get something out of this person — it was weird having someone around that she didn't know and wasn't able to talk to.

"Wait, before we go," she said in answer to the person's gesturing for her to follow. "At least tell me your name."

There was a long pause. The person turned back toward her slowly. Ember squinted into the place their eyes should be and thought that maybe she could catch the shape, the edges, of the person's eyes through the weave of the fabric.

Then, just as slowly, the person moved. Lifted one

covered hand to their face, pressed their cloth fingers to their lips, and shook their head.

"You can't talk?" Ember guessed.

The person shook their head again.

"At all?"

They shook their head.

"Oh." Ember's cheeks went warm, and not just from the heat in the air. "I'm sorry. Were you always like that?"

The person made a funny gesture with their arms, a sort of helpless little flail, then settled again and waved for Ember to follow them.

She obeyed, and they walked through the qasun in silence.

Papa was waiting for them on the far side of the courtyard. He dismissed the other person with a nod, then turned and smiled at Ember. "Shahif tells me you got caught in the storm. What did you see?"

Ember winced. As much as she hadn't wanted to talk about it with Shahif, she wanted even less to discuss her mangled, decaying hands with her father. "Nothing important. None of it was real."

"Mmm." He looked at the wall but didn't seem to see it. She wondered what he saw, if anything at all, or if he was just watching whatever his mind was playing for him.

Then, before she had a chance to ask him about it, he blinked and snapped back to the moment, smiling at her again. "Come. I've called for dinner."

Ember trailed him into another room she hadn't been in before. It was large and square, the only furnishings a long table and a couple of chairs, but that table was absolutely laden with food. Ember froze and stared at the spread, unsure if this was something else she wasn't supposed to believe was real.

Frost had food — enough, even, that there were entire

buildings where strangers offered to bring her whatever she wanted off a list full of things she'd never even heard of. Enough that one of the first things Felix had thought to do was hand her one of his own apples.

That was still astonishing. Dusk's rations were so slim and growing slimmer as the stocks ran out that Ember had trained herself long ago to ignore a rumbling belly.

In Dusk, you ate so you wouldn't die of hunger that night. In Frost, you ate to enjoy yourself.

But all that was nothing compared to this table, which nearly bowed under the weight of the food on top of it. Ember's experience with food was limited to the dry rice and occasional jerky or cafei of Dusk rations, or the small sampling of things she'd tried in Frost: apples, muffins, eggs, hot chocolate. But this was something else, more food than she could ever hope to eat or even identify. Meats and pastries, steaming pots and pots set into ice, fruits and vegetables and nuts and roots and who knew what else.

Papa grinned and waved her toward the table. He took a seat himself at one end, and Ember, still trying to see and identify all the different trays and pots and plates in front of her, followed his lead, probably just in time before her legs grew too weak with hunger and astonishment to hold her up anymore.

"This is dinner?" she asked, her voice creaking uncertainly over the words.

Papa's grin widened. "The benefit of being the prince."

Another set of footsteps came into the room, then paused much like Ember's had when seeing the table. "What the…"

Ember turned and smiled at Felix's astonishment. "Hey."

He met her eyes, and a smile of his own flickered

across his lips, almost like he couldn't help it, but it didn't entirely chase away the frown in his eyes.

Papa stood again and gave the same eager wave for Felix to join them. "There you are. I thought we might talk, and it is dinnertime. Are you hungry? Please, help yourselves."

Felix sank into the chair beside Ember but didn't reach for any of the food.

But Ember was not in the mood to properly restrain herself. The broth and water of her usual Sand meals had been good, but she ached for something to chew, and everything here smelled excellent. She wanted to sample it all, but there was so much she was sure she'd be stuffed like a pillow before she got through half of it.

One bite of everything, she decided. If she could limit herself to that, she might stand a chance.

Papa watched her with laughter glinting in his eyes as she took the tiniest samples she could manage of everything she could reach onto her own plate. "Good?" he asked at last.

Ember couldn't answer — her mouth was too full of all kinds of flavors, sweet and savory and spicy. She just nodded instead.

He glanced at Felix, who still hadn't made a move toward any of the food. "And you, son?"

"I'm not hungry."

For some reason, this made Papa cackle. "Of course you're not."

Ember swallowed her bite of one of the cold soups and struggled to pull her attention off the next one. "Felix, you should at least try something. These are really good."

He smiled tightly at her. "It's okay. I'm really not hungry."

"Not at all?"

He shook his head.

Ember set her spoon down. It occurred to her in that moment like it never had before that she'd not seen Felix eat before.

That couldn't be right — he'd taken her to a cafe once and ordered something. Surely he'd eaten then.

Except ... he hadn't. He'd offered his plate to her without touching it and didn't say anything when she ate it all.

She looked him over now with fresh curiosity. Maybe it was a Frost thing to not eat in front of others? But that couldn't be right — she'd seen Frost people eat plenty. They had cafes where people went to eat in public, where they sat outside and sipped their drinks while watching other people come and go around them.

Maybe it was just an oddity of Felix, some quirk she hadn't noticed until now because she didn't know him quite as well as she might've hoped. Knowing what she did about his father — a strange, stern man who ran the doll division of the Frost Envoys — she wouldn't put it past him to make his son shy of eating in public.

"It's fine," Felix said with another attempt at a smile. "I'm really not hungry. Don't let me stop you."

Ember didn't need further encouragement. That next plate, full of small, bright red fruits, was almost singing her name.

At last, at least Papa started reaching for some of the dishes, though his eyes remained on Felix. "Tell me about yourself, Felix. Do you have any hobbies? Interests? Things you dislike?"

"Uh ... sure. Of course."

"Such as?"

Felix hesitated, glanced down at the table like it would

offer him the answers, then back up at Papa when nothing came from the wood.

Ember swallowed the fruit — it was sweet and just a little bit tart, and so juicy she had to wipe her lips clean of the drops — and cut into Felix's floundering. "Well, there's architecture. And art. The cathedral, the old city — you wouldn't shut up about the way they made the dome for, like, three days while we were working on the copter."

Felix grinned at her. "I was just getting my revenge on you for gushing over the copters."

Ember rolled her eyes and grinned back.

Papa leaned forward, plucked a fruit from one of the plates in front of Ember, popped it into his mouth and chewed slowly. "You stole a copter from Frost."

"Well, sort of." Ember could feel her cheeks growing warm — she ducked her head and gave herself a moment by shoving a bit of meat into her mouth. "We found a bunch of them disabled in an old building, and I put one back together. It's how we got here."

"Hmm." He took another fruit from the plate, chewed and swallowed, then turned his attention back to Felix. "What is it that you like about art?"

Felix made a face, obviously uncertain, and Ember could almost sympathize. She didn't know or care a whole lot for art, but it was an odd question, like asking someone what they liked about color or how they felt about having arms.

And, underneath it all, in a place she didn't want to acknowledge because it felt silly just to let it exist, something inside her burned. She wasn't even sure what it was or why it was there, only that she felt it when her father paid Felix the attention he wasn't giving her.

She tried to concentrate on her plate, on the feast spread out before her that had, just a moment ago, been a proper distraction, but everything tasted off now. Her stomach was fuller than it had ever been, and even though she'd barely sampled half the things available to her, each bite was going down much harder than the last and hitting her stomach with an unpleasant gurgle.

She wasn't, it seemed, going to be able to try everything laid out on the table.

"Fascinating," Papa said, interrupting the unhappy turn in Ember's thoughts. "I wouldn't have expected such … well, independence, I suppose … from you. You are remarkable."

Felix fidgeted. "Um. Thank you."

Ember bit down on the inside of her lip until the pain of teeth on flesh overshadowed the ugliness she suddenly felt at Felix.

Jealousy, she realized. That was what that feeling was.

It was absurd. Felix hadn't done anything wrong, didn't deserve her feeling that way about him.

But there it was, a strange, slimy sort of feeling deep in her gut, impossible to miss and impossible to ignore.

She focused on her food, didn't let anything else cross her mind except her food. It was good, and she liked it, and the fact that Felix wasn't eating it and she was wasn't some kind of basis to compare their characters.

Papa was eating. That suggested to her that eating was the right and proper thing to do.

"I went over to the 'akhelum," she said, interrupting but not caring. "That's why I was out in the storm."

Papa turned to her. "And?"

"They wouldn't let me in, not even to see Eli."

"Mmm." Papa sighed. "Well, it was worth a try. I'd hoped they wouldn't mind letting a girl inside, that they'd think you harmless. I suppose I was wrong. Finish up your meal — I'm inclined to retire early this evening."

Ember cleaned up her plate, shot one longing look toward the dishes she hadn't been able to try, and stood. Felix joined her. "I'll let Eli know. Maybe it'll be easier for him to slip out than for you to slip in," he whispered as they turned toward the door.

Something heavy, a weight she didn't know she'd been carrying, lifted at the suggestion. "Would you?"

"Of course. Should've done it already."

They were about to exit the room, and Papa stood up, too. "Ember? Before you go, may I have a moment?"

She turned, something much brighter and sharper than those twangs of jealousy lighting her up from the inside. Papa nodded to Felix, a thank you and a dismissal together, and Felix took the hint and left.

Once he was clear of the room, Papa held out one hand to her. She took it and let him tug her into his space.

They stood in silence for a moment, the space between them growing awkward. Papa continued to hold her hand, but the angle of it was odd, twisted her wrist around so she couldn't quite get comfortable.

Finally, just as Ember was about to make comments about the weather just for something to say, Papa broke the silence. "I'm sorry I've been so distant these last days."

She shook her head. "You've been busy."

"That's no excuse for overlooking you." He dropped her hand, but only so he could put his arm around her shoulders and pull her into a hug. "I've missed you, *devushka*," he whispered, directly into her ear.

Ember buried her face into his tunic and willed away the tears that stuffed her throat. He smelled like soap and silk. It wasn't how she remembered him, but again, she pushed the thought away. They weren't in Dusk anymore — both of them probably smelled different than they used to, because now they could bathe without freezing half to death.

It didn't matter. Her cheek recognized the shape of his shoulder, even if it didn't quite fit there the way it used to. "I've missed you, too, Papa," she whispered back. Her voice caught only once.

"I know, doll. I know. It's been a long time. But we're together now, aren't we?"

Ember nodded. She couldn't swallow down the tears anymore, and a few leaked from her eyes. She wiped them away before they could stain his expensive tunic.

"Together." He wrapped both his arms around her back and pulled her in tight. "It's just you and me, just like it always was before."

"Together," she whispered back. The word felt like a promise.

At last.

Chapter Five

THEY CAME LATE THAT NIGHT, the hushed rap of fingers against her door startling her out of a restless sleep.

As soon as they were in her room, the door closed, Ember turned and hugged Eli fiercely. Words crowded her throat, all of them begging to be let out, but she kept her mouth shut and let the pressure of her embrace do the talking.

Eli hugged her back, just as tight and just as silent, and some piece of her, something jagged and broken, slotted back into place.

Frost had been difficult on them both, and for a while, Ember had been afraid that they had crossed a line their friendship could never recover from. Now, holding Eli close and feeling him do the same, Ember knew they would be all right. Maybe not perfect, definitely never the same, but all right.

Eventually, slowly, Ember stepped back, breaking their hold on each other, and looked Eli up and down. It was dark in the room, but Ember was used to the dark and not terribly concerned by it.

Eli looked good. Certainly better than the last time she'd seen him, weak and bloody from the stab wound in his gut. He was dressed like Papa or Shahif, in a long tunic that started high on the neck and dropped nearly to the ankles, and the fabric, even in the dark, seemed to gleam gently with expensive embroidery and vibrant dyes. From the fit of the cloth, she couldn't even tell he wore a bandage around his ribs, though she'd definitely felt the slight bulk of it while they hugged.

Even better, he was standing up straight, and his eyes were bright with the life she'd worried he'd lose at the queen's hands.

"Hey," she said at last.

Eli grinned. "Hey."

"Are you okay? I've been worried."

"I'm fine. Pretty great, actually. The Brothers have a healing touch."

She ran her fingers lightly across his ribs, outlining the shape of the bandage, desperate to reassure herself that it was there and doing its job of keeping him well. "There's been no fever? No infection?"

"None. Like I said, the Brothers know what they're doing."

"Good." The word came out like a sigh — of relief, of gratitude, of exhaustion.

Eli was okay. Felix had said as much before, and Ember didn't disbelieve him, but it was one thing to hear the news and another to see the reality of it right before her eyes.

Eli was okay. Healing. Here. Safe and whole.

Ember gestured toward the couch, and all three of them sat down together, close enough for knees and shoulders to touch. She reached out to both of the boys, and both of them took one of her hands in theirs.

And, for the first time in days, Ember felt safe. Finally surrounded by people she trusted, people who would look after her just as surely as she would look after them.

Felix squeezed her fingers gently. She squeezed back.

"How've you been?" she asked Eli.

It was, essentially, the same question she'd already asked, but it was also about the only thing she could think of to say. The only thing to break the quiet without cutting through that feeling of safety that had only just settled on her.

"Fine. Healing. The Brothers have been good to me."

"No question of that." She shot a look at Eli's obviously expensive tunic. "You're dressed up as nice as the prince."

Eli made a face. "I don't think that's what they were going for. The prince is…"

He faded off, obviously searching for the right word, and Ember cut in before he could come up with anything cruel.

"My father."

Eli opened his mouth, but then closed it again as the meaning of her words sank in. "What?" he managed at last.

Ember almost smiled at his tone. "I thought the same thing when I first noticed. But it's true — my father has been alive, and the prince of Sand, apparently, this whole time."

"Are you sure?"

Ember dropped his hand and leaned away from him, frowning. "What are you suggesting?"

"Nothing! It's just … that sounds kind of convenient, doesn't it? Your father is the prince of Sand, and he's keeping you locked up in his place?"

"I'm not the one being locked up," Ember shot back. "I tried to see you today, and your guard kept me away. Called me names and spat at me while he was doing it, too."

"I didn't know."

He was trying to backpedal, to return to the moment before this conversation had turned into an argument. Ember sat back into the couch, relenting, letting him do just that.

She wasn't sure where that spark of anger had come from — Eli wasn't really saying anything to deserve it. His suspicion was justified, reasonable, even if it was a touch out of his normal trusting character. Ember herself had been unsure of the whole thing, and hearing it secondhand like Eli was, she wouldn't have taken the truth of it at its face.

But Eli should believe her. She wasn't lying. She wouldn't lie — not to him. Not about that.

And why was Felix, still sitting silent at her other side, not backing her up? He'd seen Papa, talked to him, even captured his interest in a way Ember had yet to for some unfathomable reason. He could've piped in to mention the truth of her claim, so why didn't he?

Ember slumped a little farther into the couch cushions. They were soft and allowed for plenty of slumping. Maybe she wasn't quite as looked after as she might've hoped.

"They're an odd group of men," Eli said, his voice deliberately light, as if hoping to pull the tone of the moment back to something a little more friendly by force alone. "The Brothers, I mean. Spend twenty hours a day sitting around a door to an empty room and keep getting disappointed every time they open it up and find that the room is empty."

"So they're mad." This was hardly a surprise — the

man who'd confronted Ember outside of the 'akhelum had certainly been out of his mind. It wasn't hard to imagine that the rest of them inside the building might be as well.

"A bit, yeah. But they've been kind. They think I'm going to make that empty room not empty."

"What do they think should be in there?"

Eli shook his head. "Dunno. They just go on about something called the Spindle."

Ember's blood ran suddenly cold, and she straightened from her slouch at the words. "The Spindle? Do they have it?"

Eli frowned. "How do you know about the Spindle? They said no one outside the building does."

"My father is looking for it."

"And only the mustafi can find it."

It was the first thing Felix had said this whole time, and he spoke low, like sharing a secret. Ember and Eli both turned to him — he was staring out into the middle distance as if not really paying attention, or like he was trying to pay attention to a conversation that was happening on the other end of the room instead, even though there was only silence elsewhere.

Ember tugged on his hand. His fingers had gone loose around hers, but slowly, as if the effort were painful, his attention came back from that middle-distance stare. "Do you know something?"

"I … there must've been a story. Something. I recognize the words but don't actually know what they are. The Spindle. Mustafi. The new Atalanta."

"Felix…" Ember let her voice fade. She didn't actually have anything to say after that, and what she did was only to mention that what he was saying didn't make sense.

Felix smiled at her, but the smile wasn't a real one, only a strange facsimile of his usual warm expression. It tilted his lips but didn't touch his eyes, which went back to that strange unfocused look. "Sorry. I don't know what that's about. Just old stories or something. I wish I knew." He shook his head. "This place makes me feel strange."

Ember thought about the storm, hallucinations she had spent a couple of minutes feeling were real, the strange spikes of her emotions that seemed to have nothing to do with what was happening around her, and understood. Maybe Sand's strangeness manifested differently for different people, but she definitely felt it, too. She squeezed Felix's hand again. "As long as you don't strip off all your clothes and stop bathing, you're still better off than the Brothers."

Felix not-smiled again at that. Eli made an objecting noise in his throat.

"What? Don't pretend that isn't weird."

"I didn't say anything."

"You were thinking things."

Eli made another of his faces, this one a disbelieving eyeroll. "You're jumping to conclusions. They're just different."

"Crazy," Ember corrected.

Eli shook his head but didn't try to argue further. Ember knew he couldn't — she was right.

"Your father's looking for the Spindle?"

It took her a moment longer than it should've to process the words and make decent sense of them with her thoughts caught up on the Brothers.

Ember hesitated, biting her lip. She'd already said as much before, but she wondered suddenly if she should confirm it. Eli was with the Brothers, who had apparently been treating him well and hoping he could do what Papa wanted of her. She trusted Eli, of course she did — she didn't know how to live her life if she didn't trust Eli — but Sand made everything a little bit fuzzy.

If he was with the Brothers, who had kept her and, presumably, Papa away from the Spindle, was it possible that Eli might end up siding with them, against Papa? Against her?

She felt silly the moment the question crossed her thoughts. It was nonsense, the idea that Eli might not be on her side, whatever that might mean. Eli was her friend first and foremost, her brother in all but parentage. He'd crossed tundra and desert with her because neither could imagine life without the other in it.

To spite that silly paranoia, she nodded and told him even more than he'd asked. "We're going to use it to fix the Leshii. Bring the world back to the way it was Before. We're going to bring back trees. Animals. Food and warmth and balance and … and *hope*!"

Both of the boys went still and silent at the thought.

Ember had never really known hope. Perhaps Felix had, growing up in Frost where at least some light and warmth existed, where they had food enough to offer it in friendly hellos to strangers. But Ember was a child of Dusk — the last of its children. She'd spent her life scraping by on dwindling rations of light and food with no way to gain or grow more. Dusk had been doomed from the moment Before became now. She and Eli had both always known that.

Dusk was dead. The only reason people clung to survival there was because they were too stubborn to die. But there was nothing there to live for, aside from putting off starving or freezing to death until tomorrow. Hope, for a future, for the possibility of making life worth the effort, was a luxury no one could afford.

But what if she and Papa brought the Leshii back to

life? Its death was what sent their world into this grim
spiral — its revival would set it all back to the way it was
Before.

Eli let out a long, low breath. "Right. Of course I'll
help you in any way that I can."

Chapter Six

THAT NIGHT, Ember dreamed of the Leshii.

In a way, she always had been. Her father told her about the great Engine when she was only toddling, and after he left, she found some of her happiest moments at the feet of old Korrah, Dusk's oldest person and just about the only one left alive who actually remembered Before. Even before leaving for Frost, she'd been dreaming of the Leshii in some way or another.

But tonight was different. In her childhood dreams, the Leshii had been a great engine, yes, but it had been a benevolent force, creating the world Before out of the desire to see good wrought by its people.

Tonight, it wanted only destruction.

She knew even as she was watching it, trapped inside the confines of her dream, that it wasn't the Leshii's fault. The destruction it wreaked was because it was dying, struggling in a doomed effort to protect itself.

It created storms, terrible things of sand and wind and lightning that pried open the hearts of the people it touched and showed them their worst nightmares.

It created floods, washing the coastlines clean of those who had used and abused it for so long.

It created tundra and desert to freeze and melt away all the life that had been sucking it dry.

And then, when it could do nothing more, the Leshii flickered out like a candle at the end of its wick.

Ember watched it all, unable to speak or move, unable to go to the dying thing at the center of her dream and either bring it back to life or help it to a peaceful death. Only at the end of it, with the world she knew changed from Before to now, could she go over to the Leshii, rest her fingers against the rusting metal of its gears and belts, and tell it she was sorry.

Help me, she heard, as if from a voice speaking very quietly from very far away.

I will, she answered back, in that same faraway voice. *I will.*

She was startled awake by the sound of her maid coming in with breakfast.

"Godden," she mumbled to the clothed person, who nodded silently in return. Ember considered them a moment, trying to see through any part of the cloth to something that might be a face or eyes or arm or other human flesh. It disturbed her more than she quite knew what to do with that she couldn't make out any of that, that the only reason she had to think there was a person there at all was because they seemed about the right size and had arms and legs that appeared to end in hands and feet.

Which didn't actually separate them from any number of the dolls she'd seen in Frost or Sand, but the only way to really tell the difference between a doll and a person was by the dolls' unnaturally wide and permanently affixed smiles. If this person, or any of them covered in cloth, were dolls, Ember didn't think there was any way to know.

She ate her breakfast — broth and water as usual — in silence, always painfully aware of the invisible eyes on her.

But before she could finish up her meal and be left to the quiet aloneness of another day in Sand, Papa came into her room. "Ah, there you are," he said, as if Ember was likely to be anywhere else. He nodded a dismissal to the person in cloth, who immediately scurried away.

Ember set down her bowl of broth and shifted to stand, but he held up one hand and took a seat beside her instead. Slowly, as if afraid that she might try to shake him off, he reached for and took her hand, first in one, then in both, of his own.

"Ember," he said with a gravity in his tone that made Ember's breath catch in her throat. "I've been unkind to you."

Her tongue nearly tripped over itself in an effort to spit out her next word. "N-no."

"But I have. You're my daughter who I haven't seen since you were a small girl, and I haven't so much as asked you how you are."

"It's okay. I'm fine, really. Just…" Her breath caught again — she cleared her throat and pressed on before the embarrassing demonstrativeness of that could give her away. "I'm glad you're okay. I thought you'd died. Everyone did. No one survives the tundra and all."

He smiled. His teeth were almost unnaturally bright against his dark skin, like a flash of the moon through a cloudy night sky. "And yet, here we are."

"Here we are." She squeezed his hand. The gesture wasn't enough, not by half, but it was something. His use of "we" made her eyes prickle with tears.

She wanted them to be a "we." They were when she

was little, back when it was only them in the house, bundled up near the fire and looking over the precious few books he had. She didn't think they ever would be again.

To have that chance again, to be a "we," to see her father, no matter where his attention caught, what he wanted out of her or anyone else around him — it was more than Ember could've ever dreamed.

She would make him happy with her. Proud of her. She'd never really had that chance before. She was too small when he left Dusk to really appreciate what she had before, and she'd spent so long believing — knowing — that if she had been a better daughter, surely he wouldn't have left her at all.

If she'd made him proud, if she were good and useful and able to do everything he wanted of her, he wouldn't have wanted to leave.

This was her second chance. She never thought before she'd be able to have it, and now she knew she couldn't blow it.

"What have you been up to in the last years?" Papa asked, and Ember smiled with an idea.

"Let me show you."

She got up and went around the couch to the little drawer where she'd kept her compass. She'd spent the better part of many of these dull, quiet days locked up in the Sand qasun fiddling with it, taking it apart and putting it back together, trying to work out why it continued to mostly point south-ish. She hadn't figured that out, but she had managed to puzzle out many of its manufactured inner workings, and she thought that maybe, with a little bit of experimenting, she might be able to reproduce something similar.

Compasses were an artifact of Before, back when Steppe was able to manufacture ... well, anything, frankly.

Because manufactories took power, and power was something that died with the Engine, except in limited supply, like the machines of Frost. But if she could figure out the way compasses did what they did, she could figure out how to make them again.

She could, if she tried, just barely imagine a world where everyone had their own compass, a reliable way to tell one direction from another even if the sun didn't rise and the stars weren't out. People wouldn't *get* lost in the tundra, and then, perhaps, Dusk and Frost could communicate. Share resources.

Maybe, just maybe, Dusk wouldn't have to die at all.

She pulled out the compass and brought it back over to the couch to show Papa. "Do you remember this? You left it."

Papa took the little circle of metal and glass and stared down at it for a long, silent moment as the needle swung back and forth in one if its wilder displays of misalignment.

"It's broken," Ember admitted, as if that weren't perfectly obvious. "Just stopped working a few days before the doll came to Dusk."

Papa lifted his eyebrows at her, though his attention stayed on the swinging arm of the compass. "You had a doll in Dusk?"

So invited, Ember told him about the doll who interrupted her quiet life with the queen of Frost's invitation, the weeks she spent in Frost trying, unsuccessfully, to fix either the queen's dolls or her machines, her discovery that the wall wasn't cracking due to anything wrong with the machines but because it was melting from the other side, her escape in the rebuilt copter from Frost and arrival here.

Papa let her talk the whole time, only interrupting occasionally with a clarifying question. He knew some of it already, but laying it all out in order like that made it make sense to Ember at last. She'd been trapped in some kind of confused fog about it, and explaining the whats and whys of everything to her father sorted and sifted her thoughts, clarified her Frost adventure in a way she hadn't expected.

"The queen said the wall protected the city, but what it was really doing was making it impossible for the people of Frost to know what the world outside the walls is like. They don't even know Dusk exists, never mind that it's dying. They're so isolated. So cut off from any other thoughts or knowledge about the world that Felix didn't even have a concept of Before."

Papa grinned at that. His eyes had come off the compass at this latest assessment, and he studied Ember with a new warmth in his expression. "That would be Natalya's doing, I imagine."

"The queen?"

He nodded.

Ember ducked her head and smiled wryly. "I never even thought about her having a name. Silly of me."

"She doesn't want people to think of her as like them at all. Keeps herself separated and aloof like a proper goddess."

"Something like that, yeah."

"This compass. Have you ever tried following it?"

Ember blinked, momentarily thrown off guard by the sudden change in subject. "What? Like, following the point?"

Papa nodded. His eyes were back on the needle, which had stabilized a bit during Ember's story and was now pointing out the window of her room.

"No."

"Perhaps you should."

Ember fought down a scoff at the suggestion. Papa

wasn't the sort of man one scoffed at, no matter how odd the words coming from his mouth. "Why would I? It's broken, especially here. All that swinging around it does — that's new. Started here, in Sand."

He pressed the compass into her hands and then held them there, his fingers curled over hers as she held the metal, now warmed by his palm. "Ember," he said in that same serious voice that made her desperate to please him. "Just try it. For me. I think it might be trying to point to something, and I think that something may be the Spindle."

Chapter Seven

EMBER FOLLOWED Papa to the entrance of the qasun, watching the compass the whole time.

Following a compass needle only worked if it was pointing in the direction you wanted to go. But then, if it *was* pointing toward the Spindle, then perhaps it was pointing in the direction she wanted to go.

Papa nodded her toward the door and out into the desert. Ember bit the inside of her lip and refused to think about the last time she had set foot out there, caught in the storm that showed her her worst nightmare—

She shook her head, banishing the thought. The sky around them looked clear, a dusty blue in every direction. No storms to worry about.

"Go," Papa said when she hesitated. "See what you find."

It crossed her mind, fleetingly, to wonder why he was sending her when he was the one so sure and wanting to see where the compass led.

She banished that thought, too, and stepped out into the desert, her eyes on the compass.

It had settled again, and the direction it led was just to the west of the 'akhelum. Ember followed it diligently, growing confused as the needle continued to point her on a path just west of the 'akhelum.

Papa had fixated on the 'akhelum as the place where the Spindle was, and from what Eli had said, so had the Brothers. But the compass seemed to have other ideas — instead of sending her toward the building, it sent her around it.

Ember paused near the far southwestern corner of the 'akhelum. Beyond this step was desert as far as the horizon in every direction, and she wasn't prepared for a hike through the desert.

She should ask about fuel for her copter. She hadn't seen it since Shahif had taken them away from it those nights ago. With some preparation and fuel, she was sure she'd be able to take the copter farther than her own feet could carry her, keep following the compass that way.

Today, though, she only took that final step that put her beyond the far corner of the 'akhelum.

The compass needle began to spin.

Ember frowned down at it and took an experimental step back to the edge of the 'akhelum. The needle steadied. A step forward, and it began whipping around the face of the compass like the poor broken machine it was.

Ember backed up a couple of steps so the needle went quiet again. Technically, she wasn't quite following it — the needle pointed just a degree to her left, but to her left was the blank wall of the 'akhelum.

She wasn't sure when that had actually happened. The compass had been pointing her past the 'akhelum, just a little, when she first started walking this side of it. That was why she hadn't bothered to knock on the door again or otherwise try to get inside.

Ember turned around and walked quickly back the way she'd come, paying full attention to the compass now, noticing for the first time when it shifted that extra degree or two to suggest it was pointing inside the building.

There.

She stopped, turned back around so that she and the needle faced the same direction. Here, it pointed her to continue following the southwest wall — one step forward, and it tilted just that little bit to suggest she was supposed to be inside.

She looked over the place in the 'akhelum's wall. It was a nondescript patch of windowless wall, the same thick, lumpy, sand-colored wall of every building she'd seen here. She ran her fingers along the space, not expecting to feel anything but because she knew Papa would ask her about it, and she wanted to provide as much detail as she could.

As her fingers grazed the wall, sparks seemed to leap into her skin. She jumped and tried to pull away, more out of surprise than pain, but something, some kind of thrall, held her in place. Images danced before her eyes.

The Engine. The Leshii, in its full working glory. Beautiful and strange, like some kind of unfamiliar creature, gears and belts moving like muscles under a metal skin. Surrounding it was a great forest like nothing Ember had ever seen or imagined. Trees as thick as houses, taller than even Frost's tallest spires. Leaves like a blanket covering their tops, green and living. Mammals, birds, little humming insects flitted through the leaves or scuttled around the base of the Leshii.

People. So many people. They built cities full of cathedrals and libraries, bathhouses and homes, schools and shops. They flourished under the protective barrier of the Leshii. They didn't appreciate what they had. The farther out from the safety of the forest they traveled, the more they demanded of the Engine until it could no longer keep up and—

The images stopped as abruptly as they'd started.

Ember staggered back, the hand that had touched the wall buzzing with some kind of leftover energy. The compass in her other hand spun like a copter blade at takeoff.

She sucked in several breaths, realizing only as the hot air burned down her throat that she hadn't been breathing right. Though the image of the forest and the beautiful, strange engine that created it was gone, the smell of it lingered, a sort of afterimage of life. Dirt and rain and living things growing from the mulch of earlier dead things.

That had been the world Before; she recognized it from whatever descriptions of animals and plants she'd managed to glean over her lifetime. That was what had been lost with the death of the Engine.

That was what Papa was going to bring back, as soon as she could find the Spindle.

Ember spun around again and ran for the qasun. "Papa! Papa!" she yelled as shoved through the door.

Papa was standing in the hallway, speaking in a low voice to Shahif, and scowled when Ember's cries interrupted his words. "What now, child?" he snapped.

Ember pulled up short from both her shouts and her half-running steps at his tone, sharp as a slap across the face. "I think you were right," she said after a moment as he continued to glare at her. "About the compass, I mean. I think it's pointing toward the Spindle. And I think I found it."

PAPA HURRIED AFTER HER, almost taking the lead as they followed the compass back to the place Ember had touched the wall and seen the images.

"No, no, it's somewhere around here," Ember said as Papa moved a bit too far along the southwestern wall of the 'akhelum. She watched the compass with all her attention, waiting for the moment it would tilt that tiny bit toward the wall and she could show Papa what she found. She was sure it was near here, along the southwestern wall, about in the middle between the qasun and the open desert.

There. The compass didn't quite tilt the way she was waiting for, but she could make out the faint scuff of her footprints in the bits of loose sand, the place she trampled down, moved back and forth over, paused and stumbled. The wind was already stirring the sand to cover the evidence, but she was looking for it, and that was definitely it.

"Right here," she said before Papa could move farther along. She stood in the exact place she'd been just a few minutes ago and ran her fingers along the wall as she had when the images sprang at her.

Nothing.

Ember frowned, glanced down at her feet. Her sandals were in the right spot, edges matched with edges, though the edges in the sand had gone a bit soft. She looked at the compass. It wasn't quite pointing at the wall like it had at first, but that shouldn't matter — this was definitely the spot. She pressed her fingertips, then her whole hand, against the side of the 'akhelum, feeling for the spark, the sudden onslaught of images, the sense of what was behind the wall.

Still, there was nothing.

Papa frowned at her, not accusing, exactly, but definitely not pleased the way she thought he'd be.

"It was here," Ember said. She pressed her hand hard against the wall. "Right here. I *felt* it. I did!"

But had she really? Or had she confused her dreams

with a moment in reality, bumped against the wall and just remembered last night's dream?

She'd felt so sure of what she'd experienced here just a few minutes ago, but now, under Papa's expectant gaze, that surety was slipping away.

Ember dropped her hands to her sides. The empty one, the one she'd tried to feel for the Spindle with, balled into a fist, the tightness of her fingers reminding her that at least she had fingers. After the storm, the certainty of that fact at least was welcomed.

"Maybe not," she said as the silence between them stretched from expectant to painful. "Maybe I was imagining things."

It stung her to say, partly because she was usually good at telling the difference between dreams and reality, but mostly because it squelched the hopeful light in Papa's eyes, the expectation in his face.

He'd believed her when she told him she'd found something, and now she had to admit that maybe she hadn't. His disappointment, even unvoiced, tore like teeth through her, and she swallowed down the sudden urge to cry.

Papa's shoulders drooped, but his voice was soft, a low rumble beneath the endless rush of the desert wind. "Alright, no need to cry. We'll just keep looking."

Ember nodded. "Yeah. Yeah, of course."

She thought of Eli, somewhere behind the 'akhelum walls, waiting for a chance to help, too. From what she understood from their conversation last night, he knew where the Spindle was kept, even if he hadn't actually found it himself.

If she could just get inside the 'akhelum...

As if the thought summoned them, two Brothers approached her and Papa as they dithered at the wall. Both of them were just as naked and hairy as the one who'd stopped her at the door, and Ember felt herself flushing even as she pretended not to notice.

"Mikail," one of the Brothers said through an obviously tight jaw.

Papa bobbed his head toward him. "As you say."

"What are you doing here?"

Papa slung one arm across Ember's shoulders. The gesture was artful, a deliberately casual way to link her to him, and Ember shivered. "I'm showing my daughter around. Surely that's not a sin."

The other Brother, the one who hadn't spoken yet, lifted his bushy eyebrows and swept his eyes from Ember's head to her feet. "Daughter? What whore did you pay to achieve that?"

Anger prickled through her, hot as the desert air. She straightened and scowled at him, but before she could push back on any of those assumptions — that her mother was a whore, that she was a daughter of a man who *paid* for her — the first Brother lifted a hand and interrupted her. "Peace, brother," he said to his friend, and the second Brother seemed to slouch back.

"It's time for you to go, qasunfi," he added, to Papa this time. "There's nothing for you here."

Papa shrugged. "As you say. Come, Ember." He tugged on her shoulders and led them around the two Brothers, who watched them with undisguised malice in their gazes.

He lifted his voice as they started away, tossed the words back over his shoulder with disdain. "We don't want to talk to such swine anyway."

A moment later, Papa's arm was torn away from Ember's shoulders, and the first Brother pinned Papa up against the wall of the 'akhelum, his dirty hands fisted against the soft cloth of Papa's tunic, his dirty teeth bared.

Ember yelped, an involuntary little noise of surprise

and fear that she immediately hoped no one else had heard, and reached for her knife, tucked out of sight and mostly out of mind in the waistband of the loose pants she wore.

She was, after all, a Dusk girl — a young woman alone in a place where lone women were seen as easy prey. She had long ago learned to carry a hidden knife.

"Watch your tongue," the Brother hissed at Papa.

Papa didn't appear especially worried, despite the violence shimmering under the Brother's skin. He merely shoved the Brother away and brushed the wrinkles from his tunic. He glanced at Ember, and one corner of his lips pulled up at the sight of her with a bare blade in one hand. "Oh, put that away, girl. The Brothers are full of hot air and piss. No need to sully your knife on their dirty flesh."

Ember lowered her knife but didn't put it away. She eyed the Brothers, first one, then the other, but neither of them looked like they were going to attack again.

Of course, she hadn't expected that first one, and especially not from the Brother who'd told his friend to be quiet about Ember's mother, so perhaps she shouldn't believe whatever conclusions she was tempted to draw about anyone right now.

But the Brothers allowed her and Papa to go, and once back behind the safety of the qasun walls, she did actually put her knife away.

Papa turned to her halfway down the hall from the door to interior rooms. "You can perhaps understand why I've been unsuccessful so far."

Ember snorted. "I take it the Brothers don't like you very much."

"That's putting it mildly. They've been actively trying to tear me down and chase me away since I first set foot in Sand. Call me a false prophet, as if I wanted to ever be their prophet at the first." He frowned. "I'm not here to fulfill some desert cult's prophecy. I'm here for the Spindle."

"What is it, exactly?"

It was the question that had hovered at the edges of Ember's thoughts, poking her every time the word came up, but now was the first time she felt like she was able to ask it.

But Papa just shook his head. "That's not important."

Which seemed like it ought to be untrue — maybe it would help her find it to know what she was actually looking for. Was it large or small? A place or a thing? The way Papa talked about it, it somehow seemed to be both.

Ember let her gaze fall to the compass still clutched in one hand. The needle moved a little, swiping back and forth across the left half of the face in lazy, unsteady arcs.

She had found something. The compass had led her somewhere, and she'd seen the Leshii when she reached that spot. She didn't know why it was gone when she returned, but it had been there at first. She was sure of it.

At least, she thought she was sure.

Maybe.

Chapter Eight

FOR THE NEXT THREE DAYS, Ember obsessed about that spot on the 'akhelum's southwestern wall.

It wasn't particularly odd for Ember to grow obsessed with something — she had the sort of mind that, when it found a mystery, had to puzzle and pick at it until she understood everything she could about that mystery.

But the feelings that overtook her now, over that apparently unremarkable spot on the 'akhelum's wall, weren't her usual picking and puzzling. They consumed her.

For three days, she lingered there at the wall whenever she could, whenever the Brothers didn't come by to chase her off. She touched that plain bit of wall in every way she could — lightly with her fingertips, pressing hard at it with her whole body, stroking, kicking, leaning, pounding. She sat next to it for hours on end and paced near it for an equal number of hours. If there was a pattern to it, if there was some way to touch it that activated it, she was determined to find it.

Twice in those three days, she was caught in a storm, and they were both times a repeat of the horrors of the first. Ember mashed herself against the wall, her face tucked hard against the lumpy surface, her arms over her head, and clung to whatever shreds of sanity remained with her.

"It's only a dream," she recited to herself, over and over again as she watched the skin fall off her bones, choked on the scent of blood caught in her throat and nose, stared down at her mangled, decaying hands.

The storm showed her other horrors as well — during one, she watched, helpless, as the formless monsters from her worst nightmares consumed her father, chased down and killed Eli. As Felix took one look at her and ran as if *she* were the monster.

"It's only a dream," she whispered, but staring down at the mangled corpses of those she loved most made it hard to believe it, especially when an equally loud voice whispered back that it was her fault. Her fault this had happened. She should've been able to fix it, but she was useless. Powerless. Unimportant in the face of so many bigger, better, smarter people, in the face of the entire world.

No matter how she tried to tell herself it wasn't true, that the visions weren't real, they were the doing of the storm, and this storm, like all others, would pass, she wasn't able to believe that until the storm finally did go, minutes or hours after it began.

On the third day, after surviving what had to have been a couple hours of nightmares in the worst storm yet, Ember found herself curled up tight in on herself, her knees pulled as hard to her chest as she could hold them, her face pressed with pressure enough to hurt against the bones of her knees. She was weeping, though glad to find that when she wiped at her face, the tears were saltwater and no longer blood.

A hand touched her shoulder, and a voice came at her as if from across the desert. It was thick with emotion, grating against a dry throat, but still familiar. "Ember? Please, c'mon, please say something."

She cracked one eye open, prepared to snap it shut again and return to her just-a-dream mantra if something horrible met her vision, but there didn't seem to be much there. It was dark, and she was under a ceiling. Inside, then, and presumably safe from the storm.

A flash of red caught her attention. She knew that color. Not blood — not so deep a red as that — not a sunset, not a fire, but something kind of like all of those. Unique, familiar. Safe.

She slowly pulled her face out of her knees and opened her other eye to take in more of that safe, familiar color, to find it attached to a person she knew and trusted.

Felix.

"Hi." Her voice croaked, the word scratching through her throat as if it had fingernails, but it was a superficial pain that helped ground her in reality.

Felix was sitting in front of her, his face and shoulders so tense that, even in the dark of inside, she could see both visibly relax at the sound of her voice, even as rough as it was. He almost smiled. "Hi."

Another face pushed up against his. This one was also familiar, though it took Ember a moment too long to properly identify it.

"Drink this," Shahif said and touched something cool to her cracked bottom lip. A bead of moisture ran across her overheated mouth, and Ember opened her lips automatically.

Something stinging and cold hit her tongue, and she gagged and pulled away, but Shahif's other hand touched the back of her head and held her still. "Drink," he said again. "It'll help."

She didn't want to, but she couldn't resist the steady pressure between his hand behind her and the cup at her lips. The drink hurt going down, but it left a pleasant cooling feeling in its wake, and sandpaper of her throat and mind softened.

Shahif didn't release her until she'd drunk every drop of the liquid in his cup, and as he pulled away, the tense lines of a frown finally eased. "Better?"

Ember released her knees from the death grip she had around them and slowly pulled herself out of her little ball. The muscles of her back and arms and legs ached in equal parts protest and relief at the motion, and by the stiffness in her bones, she thought she might've been curled into that ball for a lot longer than the couple of minutes she remembered distinctly.

She rolled onto her back, wincing at the pain of changing position, then found that she wasn't quite ready to do anything more than lie there. She was on her couch, she thought — at least, the room looked identical to her own, the view out the window close enough to her own usual view of the qasun's interior courtyard that she was comfortable assuming it was her own for now.

Felix was leaning up against the edge of the couch, almost hovering over her, still anxious even through the relief visible in his posture at her talking and moving. Shahif, having finished forcing her to drink his beverage, was standing a little to the side, his eyes tracing up and down her again and again like he was looking for something.

Ember smiled at him. "Thank you. That did help."

Shahif nodded once, acknowledging, but didn't say anything else.

"What happened?" Felix asked.

Ember lifted her head, felt the blood rush straight out of it, and decided moving further still wasn't worth the effort. She dropped her head back against the arm of the couch. "I got caught in a storm."

"Well, yeah, but after?"

She blinked, first at him, then at the room around her. After? This *was* after.

Felix seemed to understand the expression or the thought it was meant to convey. He leaned a little closer, lifted a hand as though to touch her hair, but then let it fall to the couch cushion instead. "Ember." His voice was hesitant, uncertain. "You've been like that for three days."

She didn't need to lift her head to make the blood swirl away from it again — the words, and her own shock, did that well enough for her.

Three days? That was impossible. She'd lost some time to the storm, yes — she didn't remember at all going or being brought to her room — but three days? The storm had been, to her mind, maybe only an hour ago. She was stiff and lightheaded, weak and dry, but she'd been out in the desert and attacked by another of its nightmares. Her aches and pains, her sandy mouth and throat, the jumble of her thoughts, those made sense — she'd felt the same way after both of the other storms she'd been caught in, and neither of those had stolen three days away from her.

"We were worried that you wouldn't wake up at all," Felix said, and his voice caught on the last words. "Shahif said some people don't."

Ember glanced at Shahif again, who gave another silent acknowledging nod at that news.

"Well, I did," she said, because she didn't like seeing Felix so upset. "I'm sorry, I didn't know…"

She didn't have an end to that statement; she let it fade into nothing.

"No one does," Shahif said. He moved then, turning toward the door and starting out of the room, then pausing. "I'll be back with more medicine in an hour. I have it brewing."

Ember winced at the thought of drinking more of his drink, but it did help, just as he said it would, so maybe she should be grateful.

Felix smiled at him. "Thank you."

Shahif gave another of those short nods and left, closing the door behind him.

Ember stared up at Felix. Worry still lined his face. "Three days? Really?"

He nodded. "Sometimes you were screaming or weeping, but mostly you were just lying there, and I thought—" His voice cracked. He cleared his throat and began again. "Shahif said that was normal, but he also said that some people don't survive it. He wouldn't say how many, but it sounded like a lot."

"I'm sorry. I really didn't even know."

"That's what Shahif said."

He lifted his hand again like he wanted to touch her but wasn't sure if he was allowed. She grabbed it and held it between both of her own, linking her fingers into his and settling the whole knot of them beneath her chin. His hand was warm, and even though Ember knew her own skin was sun-scorched and sand-scoured, her fingers felt cold against the healthy warm of Felix's.

Felix sighed, long and deep like he'd been holding his breath for three days, closed his eyes, and leaned his forehead against the arm of the couch, and Ember didn't mind one little bit that that motion put his head close enough to hers that, if she turned just a little, she could press her nose into his hair.

She wanted to try it. She'd been wondering since the first time she saw him if his hair would be hot to the touch, if it might burn her like fire if she ever worked up the nerve to try, and even though she knew that was a silly idea — just because his hair was the color of heat and light and fire didn't mean it would have any of the other properties of it — it had been her first thought about him, and it never had quite gone away.

In truth, after discovering that he was warm to the touch, the wondering about his hair had stuck around that much more insistently.

She ached to try it. It wouldn't take much. A tilt of her head, a little slide to the right, and she could press her nose, and maybe even her lips, right into those strands. She sensed, in some deep-down way that she couldn't quite understand but knew to be true, that the gesture, the motion from her, would be accepted. Perhaps even welcomed. Wanted just as much as she wanted to make it.

But before she could work up the nerve to make those little adjustments to her position, Felix lifted his head again, and her chance vanished. "What were you even doing out there?"

Memories spilled back into her, the whole reason she'd gone to the 'akhelum in the first place coming back in a rush. "Oh! I think I found where the Spindle is. It's inside the 'akhelum, but sometimes I can feel it from the outside—"

"All that for a *spindle*?" Felix interrupted, and now he sounded angry. "Ember, you can get those in the courtyard!"

"No, no, not like a spinning spindle." At least, she didn't think so. "No, it's … I think it's part of the Leshii.

The Engine. Papa's been trying to find it, and *I found it*. I just can't get to it."

"Ember." His voice was still angry, and his grip on her hand tightened. "You can't … you can't be going outside like that."

Ember tried to sit up, but the black spots that tangled up her vision warned her not to. She growled low in her throat and slumped back down. "I don't like being trapped behind walls."

She thought Felix would know that. Understand that. They'd brought down Frost's walls for that very reason, hadn't they?

That he made a good point — Sand storms did seem to be stopped by the walls of the qasun — was not the point. Walls were the enemy. The way people in control of those inside them kept them from understanding the world. Walls kept people brainwashed. Kept people from asking what was beyond them. Allowed dictators to be and stay in charge.

But Felix didn't rise to her bait. He just squeezed her fingers tighter. "Ember, please, please be careful. I don't…" He hesitated, cleared his throat again, pressed on. "I don't like thinking that you're going to die."

She softened. It was impossible not to with him. Eli, she could push back against, argue with, probably forever. He was as stubborn and unmovable as she could be, and he was almost always convinced that he was right.

But Felix just cared about her. If he pushed back against what she wanted to do, it was because he was worried about her getting hurt, not because he wanted to stop her from doing things.

She squeezed his hand back. She did like it there, between hers, warm and safe. She liked it when Felix touched her. She liked it when she touched him back.

"I'm sorry," she said softly, squeezing his hand again just because she liked it. "I'm here. I'm okay."

Felix nodded. The motion was a little bit jerky. "Me, too. I'm sorry. I'm not … I just…"

"I know. It's okay."

He sighed and leaned his head against the arm of the couch again, this time facing her. He looked at her, and he was so close that Ember could see the blue-gray color of his eyes even in the dark of the room.

"You're the best thing that's ever happened to me," he whispered at last. "I don't want to lose you."

Chapter Nine

EMBER DIDN'T LEAVE her couch for another day, sleeping in short fits of barely restful darkness that kept insisting on giving her nightmares.

Shahif came and went throughout the day with more cups of his drink. He called it medicine — mostly, it seemed to be some kind of cold, bitter tea. "To calm the mind and heal the body," he said when Ember, on her third administration, asked about it.

She was feeling well enough by then to sit up and hold the cup herself, so Shahif didn't have to feed her like a stubborn child. She sniffed the cup but couldn't identify the smell.

"Valerian, linden, and licorice," Shahif added, more helpfully this time.

Ember had never heard of those things, but as the tea did seem to be helping, she drank it all, doing her best to not wince at the taste.

The person all wrapped up in cloth came and went at their normal times, too, with their usual tray of water and broth. Once, they came in while Shahif was watching

Ember drink his tea, and both Shahif and the other person froze for a moment as if surprised to be seen by the other.

Shahif recovered first. "On you go, woman."

The clothed person set down the tray but didn't linger as usual to watch Ember take her meal.

Once they were gone, Ember couldn't help but ask. "Is it a woman under there?"

Shahif's expression did something complicated Ember wasn't sure how to parse. It settled at last into a tight-lipped smile. "The women of cloth. Yes, all of them are women. Or, at least, they were."

"Were?"

"They have all displeased their husbands in some way. Many of them were unable to have children. Hence why they must cover up, to hide their shame. They serve word-lessly as penance."

Ember frowned. She didn't like the idea that being unable or unwilling to have children shamed someone, or made them less than women. That if she ever admitted to someone in Sand that she herself wasn't interested in having children, she would perhaps be required to hide herself and hope someday to be forgiven. That Shahif might think about her with the same disdain as coated his voice now, inspire the same complicated, unhappy expression that crossed his face when she asked about the woman who served her meals.

She drank the rest of her tea in silence but then found that she wasn't interested in eating the broth the woman of cloth brought her. Instead, she nestled back down into her couch, tired from sitting up, and closed her eyes.

Felix remained a near constant by her couch. Mostly he stayed quiet, letting Ember rest and Shahif give his medicine, leaving only for a few minutes at a time to, presumably, eat something or relieve himself, but Ember didn't press about what he was doing when he wasn't with her. It didn't matter — he was never gone for long, and he returned to his spot leaning against the edge of the couch.

"You can come up here," Ember offered at one point, sliding down to make room for him. "The floor can't be comfortable."

But Felix shook his head. "I'm fine." He shifted a little so he was leaning his temple against the arm of the couch and smiled at her. "You need to rest."

It was sometime near midday at this point — the noise from the courtyard outside her window had died down a bit in the space between the morning and evening activities, when people in the qasun hid inside from the unrelenting midday heat. Ember had drunk more of Shahif's tea in the morning than maybe she'd drunk water in her entire life, and now she wondered if her mouth and throat would permanently taste of its bitter flavor.

She was still weak from three days of … well, whatever it was the storm had done to her, but was now feeling well enough that that weakness was starting to annoy her. "I'm tired of resting," she said, but, frustratingly, she couldn't quite bring herself to get up.

Felix smiled again, the soft one she liked best, and held out his hand. Ember took it and, though she thought she'd be embarrassed to admit it, just that one little gesture suddenly made the idea of lying on this couch a bit more bearable.

Ember rolled onto her side so she was facing him straight, settled herself a little more comfortably, and trailed the fingers of her free hand across the back of Felix's. She was fascinated by the patterns of veins beneath his skin, the tiny little bones that made up his knuckles, the faint dusting of reddish-gold hair.

He had beautiful hands. She thought about the way

he'd sometimes touched the stones and artwork inside Frost's old cathedral, the reverent graze of fingertips he seemed unable to help, and wondered what else he'd touched with his beautiful hands. What else he might graze his fingers across like they were prayer beads for Atalanta.

Whether she could somehow be one of those things.

"Tell me a story," Ember whispered into the quiet.

Felix shook his head. "I don't know any stories."

"That's not true. Tell me about Atalanta."

"You know that story. Everyone knows that story."

She smiled. "But I want you to tell it. I only know the Dusk version. Tell me the Frost one."

"You're an odd girl, you know that?" But he said it fondly, and after that told her about Atalanta, the mother of Steppe, and her discovery of the Engine.

Ember watched him through it, watched his face and his hand, and kept trying to map the little nest of veins that ran across the back of his hand, wondering if she studied them long enough, maybe she'd be able to memorize them.

She thought perhaps she might.

"She found other engines, too, you know," Ember added when Felix finished off his own tale with the awaking of the Leshii. She was sleepy now, lulled just to the edge of consciousness by the familiar story in his quiet voice.

"Yeah?" He didn't believe her, but that was okay. They were safe here, just the two of them. The couch comfortable, and Ember's eyes were so heavy.

"Mm-hm. Seven more, they said. Bet they're all just as beautiful."

"No doubt," he agreed softly, humoring her.

"Stay."

There was a pause, a faint rustle like of shifting cloth,

and just as Ember slipped over the edge into sleep, she thought she felt warm fingers touch her hair. "Of course."

By THE NEXT MORNING, she was feeling better. Between Shahif's strange cold teas and the day spent resting, Ember didn't think she needed to be kept in anymore.

Shahif disagreed. "You're only just back on your feet," he said when he came in carrying another cup to find her in the fresh clothes brought by the woman of cloth and fetching her compass for another chance at the 'akhelum walls.

"I'm back on my feet," Ember said. "That's enough."

Shahif shook his head. "It certainly isn't. Your mind—"

"Is my own, to do with as I see fit," she interrupted before he could accuse her of being weak, or broken, or whatever word he was about to use for her. "Right now, I'm going to use it to get into the 'akhelum."

The Spindle was in there, she was sure of it. She just had to figure out a way to get in. There'd been no word from Eli, not even one from the three days she'd spent curled into a ball, or yesterday when she was conscious again.

Ember hated thinking that she couldn't trust him anymore, that he wasn't going to keep his promise to help her, that maybe someone had been able to turn him against her, but those thoughts were for another day anyway. For after she and Papa fixed the Leshii and saved the world.

She slid the compass into her pocket. Sand garments, as a rule, didn't have pockets, but it had been easy enough for her to stitch one into the folds of the tunic, and so far, no one had complained about her alterations. It didn't matter if they did, frankly — pockets were necessary, and if Sand folk didn't think so, well, they didn't know what they were missing.

She was about to walk past him, but Shahif caught her arm as she did. His grip was gentle but firm, unignorable. She stopped moving and turned toward him, not sure if she was about to ask him what was wrong or insist that he let her go and never dare touch her again.

But both urges died in her throat when she caught the look on his face, that same worried frown she'd seen off and on throughout the day yesterday.

"He's not your friend, Ember," Shahif said, his voice dropping to a conspiratorial whisper.

"Who?"

"None of them. And especially not the prince."

Ember pulled her shoulder out of Shahif's grip, but gentler than she might've for the sincerity of his expression.

Shahif didn't mean her ill. She believed that. He wouldn't have taken such pains yesterday to help her if he wished her harm.

But that didn't mean she trusted him. Especially when he was talking about people he himself didn't know.

"And you think you are my friend?"

"Yes."

She stepped back, lifted her chin. "You're not."

His lips pressed tight. He offered her his cup, which she carefully didn't even look at lest he think he could continue to presume anything about her, or himself, or the nature of their relationship.

He was no one. Some qasun functionary — she hadn't quite figured out the structure of people here, so wasn't entirely sure where Shahif fit into it, but it didn't really matter. He did as her father bid, and that made him lower than her father.

At best, Shahif was a faithless adviser. At worst, a traitor.

Ember didn't suffer traitors.

"Let me pass, Shahif," she said, her voice sharp and unwavering, not quite her own, "or the prince of Sand will know about this."

He hesitated as if torn between whatever impulse he had to try and turn her against her father and the threat of her father finding out about it. After a moment, he caved to the threat of the latter and stepped aside, but not without hissing to her as she brushed by.

"Be careful, *alahziz.*"

She kept walking.

Chapter Ten

EMBER WALKED AROUND THE 'AKHELUM.

It was a pointless exercise. She knew where the Spindle was, or at least where it was most findable from the outside, but she walked around the 'akhelum anyway, not even pausing at that blank spot on the southwestern wall that tugged at her attention like it had an audible voice.

She needed to get in. There had to be a way to get in.

Could she sneak through a window? Dig a hole into a wall? Stab the Brothers who guarded the door?

She didn't feel much like getting close enough to one of the Brothers to properly stab them. The smell of them both times she'd come within smelling distance had lingered in her nose and throat long after they'd gone, and she wasn't keen on repeating the experience.

Besides, stabbing was usually unnecessary. She'd much prefer finding some other, less violent way into the 'akhelum.

The problem was, there didn't seem to be any.

The 'akhelum completely lacked windows. This wasn't surprising, exactly — Dusk houses didn't have windows, either, and she'd only gotten to thinking buildings should because Frost loved its windows, and her own room had one. But her window was inside the qasun, looking out on the enclosed courtyard. The outside walls of the qasun didn't have windows, either, she presumed to keep sand and storms out.

But it did make getting into the 'akhelum that much more difficult. Windows, she could use, either to crawl through or to at least talk to Eli and get him to let her in.

Without them, she was stuck with the door. Only one door, the one facing the qasun, where a Brother's eye peered out at her through the little peephole both times she passed it.

On her third round, the Brother spoke. "What are you doing here?" His voice was muffled by the door, but he compensated for that with his excessive volume.

Ember thought about stopping, answering, trying to draw the Brother out. Maybe, if she could get him to step a little away from the door, she'd be able to dart around him?

But that plan felt less sure than she liked, and would probably end up with her needing to stab someone, and that was what she was trying to avoid.

So, instead, she just flashed the Brother her brightest smile and kept going.

This time, on her third time round, she did stop at the southwestern wall, out of sight of the door and, hopefully, the gaze of the Brothers beyond it. There was no obviously easy way into the 'akhelum, that much was clear.

Well, she hadn't expected there to be anyway. If there were, surely her father would've already managed it.

Ember ran her fingers along the 'akhelum's lumpy brown wall, letting them skim and bump across the surface as she followed it. She hadn't taken the compass out of her pocket — she knew the spot where the Spindle was by both sight and touch at this point. She'd been pacing around it for three days.

Three days of trying to find it again. Three days of whatever had happened to her after the last storm. One day of recovering from those three days. It had been a week since she first found the Spindle, and she still didn't even know what it was.

Her fingers found the spot, and something sharp and electric jolted through them. Ember gasped and pressed her palm against the wall.

It was there. Right there, and she couldn't reach it.

There were no visions today, no memories of a working engine or the time Before. Not even the destruction of it, the horrible death rattle that had plunged the world into what it was now. Only that spark of recognition, that pull that lived somewhere deep inside her chest, that she had long ago taught herself to ignore.

But it had always been there, light as an eyelash most of the time, but *there*. Sometimes it came as hunger and mostly went away when she ate her daily ration of rice and weak tea. Sometimes it came as loneliness, and she escaped her empty home for Eli's, and they would sit together in candlelit dark and talk about whatever little nothings had happened that day. Sometimes it came as a wave of despair, a voice louder than her own thoughts that told her there was nothing, nothing she could do, nothing worth struggling for, nothing but nothing on the other side of Dusk's endless winter nights, and she would curl up under her blankets and cry until she couldn't keep her eyes open anymore.

It had always been there, and now, now, she finally understood what it was. That pull, that sensation, that voice — it was the Spindle.

It was the Leshii.

Ember pressed her other hand to the 'akhelum wall too, then, when that wasn't enough, her whole front so her forehead and chest and hips and even her toes were crushed up against the wall. Her breaths bounced back at her face, uneven and cracking with tears. "I'm here," she whispered, as if there were any chance of anything hearing her through the wall. "I'm here."

Help me.

It wasn't a voice, not really, but that was how her mind interpreted the feeling, the sudden rush of helpless terror, the soundless shriek of pain and despair that burned through her. It tore the sobs right out of her throat so she was dry-heaving against the 'akhelum wall.

Help me.

"How do I find you?"

Help me.

"I will. I *will*! I'll figure it out. I'm coming."

There was no other answer.

She had to get in. There had to be some way through, the door or the walls or something.

She marched back to the door, and this time rapped on it. The Brother's eye peered out at her. "What?"

"I need to talk to Eli."

The Brother made a low noise in his throat, though what that noise was, she couldn't actually tell. "No chance."

"Shouldn't be that his decision to make?"

The peephole closed, and the Brother didn't answer her. Ember banged on the door, first with one fist, then with both.

She got no answer.

"Open up!" she yelled.

Nothing.

With a shout of frustration, she shoved herself away from the door. It was useless — if she wanted to get into the 'akhelum, it would have to be some other way.

What she needed was for Eli to come out. Talk to her. Prove that he wasn't falling in too deep with whatever was happening to him inside this building.

He'd promised to help — she had to find a way to hold him to that promise.

EMBER COULDN'T SLEEP that night. She felt like she'd been sleeping for days and still unable to find rest in it, probably because she had been, and now, she couldn't so much as lie down long enough to get relaxed. Her limbs felt jittery, and her thoughts wouldn't settle.

She had never been more grateful for the soft rap of fingers against her door. Felix, when he came into her room, brought some of that unfocused energy something to concentrate on.

Ember glanced around the hall before she shut the door, surprised to find the woman of cloth perched unmoving near her door. For a cold second, Ember thought she was dead, despite the fact that there was no obvious wound cutting through the cloth, no blood staining her clothes or the ground around her. But then the woman shifted, just a little, and her head rolled toward her other shoulder.

Not dead, then. Asleep. Ember grinned to herself and closed the door, softly to keep from waking her guard.

Felix stood in the center of her room, his eyes locked on nothing, his expression strange and distant. She stepped over to him, that same cold rush of uncertainty flooding her again, harder.

"Felix?"

He blinked once, smiled a smile that was not his own, and shook his head like knocking away unwelcomed thoughts. "Sorry. This place…"

Ember nodded, understanding, as his words trailed into silence. Her difficulty concentrating had come as restlessness and unpredictable moods, but Felix was hardly the first person she'd seen staring blankly into the middle distance here. She tried not to notice it much, but it seemed even the dolls who wandered the qasun courtyard had similar troubles thinking straight.

Dolls didn't even think, so she was sure that meant it was normal for people to get distracted and unsure here.

"I talked to Eli."

Ember gestured for them to sit to give her hands something to do, her brain a moment to catch the full meaning of his words. "When? How? I keep trying, but the Brothers won't let me."

They sat. She picked at imaginary threads on her tunic.

"The Brothers are going to be out of the 'akhelum tomorrow night. Some ritual they perform every month. Tomorrow night's your chance to get in."

She probably should've been grateful for the news, but all she felt was frustration. "I can't wait that long."

"You've been waiting for weeks."

"That's not…" But it was, wasn't it? Ember slumped into the couch cushions and kicked at the air, a useless gesture.

Useless. Just like everything she did, everything she tried. Useless.

"You don't understand. This isn't … it's like…" But neither of those were right, either. She made a noise low in her throat, not a word or a grunt, but some painful combination of the two, and stared up at the ceiling.

Felix didn't say anything, but she could feel his eyes on her face, watching. Waiting.

"My father disappeared when I was seven," she said to the ceiling. "I thought he was dead. He's been dead most of my life. And now he's here, and he's alive, and I have a chance to help him do something. Something important. And it's not just Papa — it's the Leshii."

She turned then, back to Felix. She wanted to reach for him, take his hand, maybe finally let her fingers stray toward that impossible hair, but she pressed her restless hands together and jammed them between her knees instead. "I've been ... pulled toward it my whole life, and it's only now that I actually figured out what it is. This is what I'm meant to do, and I can't do it because some crazy desert cult has it locked up behind its walls."

"Ember," Felix began, but he cut himself off, or maybe he didn't have anything else to say after that.

She liked it when he said her name like that, soft and careful and just a little bit worried. Not that she liked that Felix was worried, but it still lit something inside her, made her feel like he *cared*.

"Tomorrow night," he said at last. "The Brothers will be gone, and Eli's going to meet you at the door."

Chapter Eleven

THE WAIT WAS AGONY.

Ember hated waiting on a good day — waiting meant there was something she was supposed to be doing but wasn't able to do yet. It meant that she was being useless, and nothing made her feel more useless than being trapped inside a single small room just waiting for time to go by.

And this day was far from a good day. On a good day, there would be something else to do, something else that could grab and hold her attention so she could at least pass the time not just agonizing over how long it was until her wait was done.

But there was nothing like that available today.

Ember paced her room. She sat on the couch and watched the people in the courtyard. A couple of times, she took herself out to the courtyard, hoping that something out there would be a distraction, but there was nothing — most of the people were dolls, and not even poorly functioning ones she could maybe open up and look inside.

She was a little bit familiar with the insides of dolls'

heads, after the weeks she spent trying to figure out why Frost's dolls were malfunctioning like they had been. For a while, she wandered around the courtyard, imagining what the inside of this doll or that one might be like, wondering if she could convince Papa to show her some things about them.

He was their inventor. Ember hadn't quite put it all together like that before, but watching them now, wondering if she could convince him to show her how they worked, did actually bring her to the conclusion she should've had the first time she saw dolls in Sand.

The prince of Sand was her father, and also the person who'd been screwing with the dolls' programming back in Frost. That made her father the unknown developer she'd seen on the dolls' programming logs.

Pride ran through her, tugged at the corners of her lips, spread a pleasant warmth into her jittery limbs. Her father had created the dolls. She'd always known he was a scientist, but dolls were something special. Mechanical people, virtually indistinguishable from real people, especially here in Sand where they didn't all walk around with those unwavering smiles on their faces.

Her father wasn't just a scientist — he was a genius. And together, they were going to change the world.

If only night would come.

It did, eventually. Ember had lived through weeks that felt shorter.

She wasn't entirely sure when at night she was supposed to approach the 'akhelum. Felix hadn't elaborated on exact times. But that was okay — she wasn't keen on waiting a moment longer than she had to, and she was standing near the 'akhelum the moment the sun had slipped beneath the horizon.

She didn't knock. Because she didn't know when the

Brothers were all going to be away, she didn't want to risk alerting them before they'd gone, so she went to her usual spot along the southwestern wall to check on the Spindle.

It wasn't there.

She paced around, ran her fingers across the wall, waited for that little pull inside her to point her in the right direction, but nothing she did inspired the arrival of the Spindle. She checked her compass. The needle swung lazily back and forth across the face, never settling on any particular direction.

Ember frowned. Even in the times when the Spindle wasn't reachable, the compass had always mostly fixed on a direction. She'd started to assume that the compass just always pointed toward the Spindle, wherever the Spindle felt like hiding. But the compass wasn't picking a direction at all now. It wasn't even spinning with the energy that usually meant she'd walked past the spot.

She shook the compass, lightly at first, hoping to realign it to the Spindle again, but then with force when it continued its lazy swinging. The pieces inside, the little gears and bits that kept the compass working, rattled slightly as if protesting her abuse.

But the needle didn't settle.

It was growing dark. Ember started toward the door.

And walked straight into a whole group of Brothers.

THE LEAD BROTHER banged on the qasun door. Ember fought against the grip another had on her, but struggling only made the twist in her elbows shoot pain all the way up and down her arm.

She wouldn't have guessed it just by looking at them, but the Brothers — at least the one holding her — were strong. Stronger than she'd given them credit for. The one standing behind her, holding both her arms tight behind her back, had a grip that might as well been made of metal for all the good struggling against it did.

"Open up!" the lead Brother shouted at the door. "Open up before we break the door down!"

From anyone else, Ember would think that an empty threat. But from the Brothers, she worried it might not be.

And apparently, someone inside the qasun agreed with her, because the door opened at the Brother's next knock, and Shahif peered out. His eyes widened visibly when they landed on Ember.

Ember smiled bitterly but didn't trust her voice.

The lead Brother wasn't interested in letting her talk anyway. He took one look at Shahif and spat, not at his feet like the Brothers mostly had at Ember or Papa, but at his face. A glob of spittle smacked Shahif on the cheek. He winced but didn't reach up to wipe it away.

"Traitor," the Brother hissed.

"What do you want?" Shahif asked in return.

"Oh, spend a few years as a qasunfi, and now you think you can order me about?" The Brother spat again, but this time at the ground, forcing Shahif to shift aside lest he end up with a glob of spit on his foot, too.

Ember squirmed against her captor's hold, and again found it did no noticeable good in freeing her hands — all it did was make her elbows feel like they were one wrong shift away from popping.

Shahif's words came out through his teeth. "What do you want, Ahli?"

"Your prince" — Ahli hissed the words with unmistakable disgust — "is violating our agreement. We found his *eahira* lurking around our walls again."

Ember didn't know the word, but the way Ahli spoke it left no question that it was an insult. She wondered if she could spit with enough force and distance to hit him, but the creaking pain in her elbows warned her against trying it.

Shahif looked at her for a long, silent moment, his gaze intense and thoughtful. Ember wasn't sure what he was seeing, but whatever it was, it made him straighten and turn that same thoughtful gaze on Ahli. "You're mistaken. The boy's not the one you're looking for — she is."

Ahli barked a single-syllable laugh, and the other four Brothers with him echoed the sound. "So, you've let the false prince poison your thoughts." He spat again, and this time it hit Shahif between the eyes. "Traitor."

Shahif wiped his eyes. The motion was strangely calm, although his face was turning red with repressed feeling. "Let her go."

Ahli made a noise in his throat, but turned to the Brother holding Ember's arms and nodded. He released her, and Ember yanked away from him, her fingers tingling as feeling rushed back down from her elbows.

"The next time I see either of your faces, I'll treat you like traitors deserve. My ax hasn't tasted blood in far too long," Ahli said.

"Understood," Shahif answered. "Now get out before I fetch the dolls."

The Brothers stepped back, leaving Ember free to go into the qasun, and Shahif slammed the door between them.

He stared at the inside of the door for a moment, the defiant calm of his previous demeanor slipping into slump-shouldered defeat. Then, slowly, he turned back to Ember. Saliva still glistened on his cheek and beneath his eyes; he wiped it away with the underside of his sleeve. "You all right?"

Ember rubbed at her left elbow, where the pressure of

her restraint had hurt the worst, trying to dig into and massage away the pain. "I'm fine."

Physically, it was true, but her thoughts were spinning again, faster than a copter blade.

The Brothers were supposed to have been out of the 'akhelum tonight, and it was Eli who was meant to meet her at the door. But those Brothers had known she was there, despite the fact that she'd avoided the door and there were no windows. They'd come as a group — not all of them, but enough — as if they'd known how many it would take to make sure Ember had no real chance of getting away from them.

They couldn't have known her intentions for the night — unless someone told them.

And Shahif knew the Brothers. She wanted to think that was just because they lived in the same area, that they'd met before and knew each other the way everyone knew everyone else in a small area, but that wasn't true. Ahli had called him a traitor. Said he'd lived a few years in the qasun and thought now he could order him about.

They knew each other, and not just because Sand was a small place where everyone knew everyone.

Was Shahif a Brother underneath his qasunfi disguise?

"Ember?"

Her father's voice cut through the confusion swirling through Ember's head. She turned to him, for a moment relieved that Papa was here. He'd help her straighten it out. He'd know what to do.

But that relief and hope withered immediately when she saw him. His eyes burned, and he came toward her with a speed like aggression, shoving past Shahif to grab her shoulder and shove her back against the wall. His voice was low, barely more than a growl, and angrier than she'd ever heard anyone before.

"What did you do?"

"Papa—"

He shoved her back again, and her head thumped against the wall, not very hard, but the shock of it sent ice running through her veins, tears thrumming behind her eyes.

"You told them."

"I—"

"Little harlot! I trusted you!"

"I didn't—"

Another shove. This time, it properly hurt when her head collided with the wall, and a couple of tears shook loose from her eyes.

"And now you're going to cry. Serves me right for expecting anything more of a woman."

"Mikail," Shahif began, but then Papa turned on him, too.

"And you. Traitorous scum. Am I to understand you've been working with *them* this whole time?"

His voice, shouting now, was pulling an audience toward them. A couple of dolls, smiling vaguely, but without the endless brightness they had in Frost, mingled with the human men and even a couple of women of cloth — including, Ember thought, the one who'd been looking after her the last couple of weeks.

"I should send you both out to the desert," Papa said, loud enough to be heard by everyone peering into the hall. "Let the monsters and the storms have you."

Ember's eyes and head throbbed in time with her heartbeat. It was all she could do to not drop right to her knees.

"But." And now Papa glanced around as if noticing his audience for the first time. The dolls watched him, their expressions unchanging, and the people watched him, too, their expressions unreadable.

He straightened, smoothed down his expensive tunic, and smiled insincerely around him. "But perhaps that's a bit harsh and neglects mercy. You may see yourselves to your rooms instead."

Chapter Twelve

THE MOMENT the door to her bedroom clicked shut behind her, Ember's fear and confusion morphed to fury.

The Brothers had been expecting her. Waiting for her.

Someone had told them. Warned them she was coming and what, exactly, she meant to do.

But no one had known, except…

She hated to think it. She'd trusted Eli her entire life, and yes, things had gotten strained and odd between them since leaving Dusk, but that shouldn't be reason enough for him to betray her trust. It certainly wasn't enough for her to do so to him. Nothing would be reason enough to betray him.

Or so she'd once thought. Now, facing a reality where Eli might have told the Brothers what she was doing, when she was going to do it, maybe even why, she wondered if that was true. Was there something she'd be willing to betray Eli for?

Maybe. Her father, or—

A soft knock interrupted her thoughts. She wheeled toward the door, wrenched it open. "What?"

Felix stood on the other side of the door. He blinked, startled by the venom in her tone. "I thought you'd want to know that the Brothers are gone."

If it had crossed Ember's mind at all that Felix was the one who'd told them, those doubts were gone. He wouldn't be at her door, telling her it was time, if he'd had anything to do with it.

That left only Eli. She'd suspected it already, but the confirmation hurt like a knife in the gut.

Maybe it was better to never trust anyone — only those you trusted could betray you.

She swallowed down her tears and lifted her chin. It wasn't the Brothers she wanted to see now.

She didn't wait for Felix, though she could hear him hurrying after her. She marched through the qasun, and something in her expression must've alerted some of the others to either her feelings or her intentions, because the courtyard went quiet behind her as she walked through it. Out the door and into the small stretch of moonlit desert between qasun and 'akhelum.

The 'akhelum door was locked up tight. She banged on it anyway. "Eli!" she screamed, and her voice was loud enough to echo across the endless desert beyond Sand's two buildings. "Get out here before I break down the door!"

She could feel Felix's frown trained on her face, the uncertainty radiating off him as he waited, curious and confused, a step behind her.

Ember ignored him. She banged on the door again, hard enough to rattle it in its frame.

There was a slight pause, then the click of a lock, and Eli peered out from the sliver of opened door. "Ember, what are you doing?" he asked, his own voice little more than a whisper. "They'll hear you."

Ember stared at her friend — her former friend. He was still dressed in finery, his own face and hair clean and neatly trimmed so he looked and smelled not only not like a Brother, but not even like himself. The Dusk that had clung to his edges, in his black always-in-need-of-a-trim mop of hair, the smoky-sweet smell of fire and sweat that lived deep in his skin, was gone, replaced by soap and the cloying-sweet of some kind of perfume. Even his face looked different, rounder than she'd seen it before, without the gauntness that came from a meager diet of too little rice and weak rebrewed tea.

This wasn't Eli. This was some stranger who had taken Eli over.

Ember ignored the invitation of the open door and grabbed Eli by his stupid gold-embroidered collar. One hard shove had him pinned by the throat against the door frame. "Traitor!" she growled, and for a moment, she sounded so like Ahli had to Shahif that she pushed Eli a little harder against the wall to chase away the sensation. "I trusted you."

"What are you—"

She cut him off with her forearm against his neck, choking his protest into silence. "Don't pretend you don't know."

"I don't!" he hissed. His throat bobbed against her arm as he tried to swallow and couldn't.

"This was my chance, and you…" She was shaking so hard she could barely draw a breath. "You ruined it!"

Eli shoved her off him and glared. "What's wrong with you?"

"Nothing." This was a lie — she said it anyway, not caring what Eli thought of her anymore. "You're the one who's changed."

Again, the thought hurt. Eli wasn't supposed to be the

one capable of becoming what he shouldn't. He was the dependable one, the even-tempered, reliable one.

And yet…

And yet, apparently all he needed was a fancy tunic and some awful perfume, and he'd do whatever he could to keep it.

"Ember—"

She hit him. Her fingers had been balled into fists this whole time, mostly to hide the way they were rattling hard enough to fall apart, and her fist caught him square in the mouth.

She launched her other fist at him, too. This one smacked into his cheek.

And then she was screaming, curses and obscenities, every foul word she could think of whether they meant what she was trying to say or not, and her fists kept hitting him, in the face and throat and shoulders, wherever she could reach. He tried to catch them, hold her still, but she ripped her arms out of his grip before he could get a solid hold and kept hitting him.

Arms circled her from behind, catching her own arms and stilling the flail of her fists. She tried to turn, but her feet came off the ground, and she lost all her leverage. She screamed and writhed, but the arms were bands of iron, unbreakable, inescapable, and the door to the 'akhelum slammed shut between her and Eli.

The arms carried her away, ignoring or not caring how Ember flailed. She couldn't get in a good hit on them, and even when she did manage to make contact with her feet or fists, her strikes didn't seem to bother the person.

She wasn't even sure who it was carrying her — they held her facing away from them and moved like she weighted nothing at all at a quick and steady pace away from the 'akhelum toward the far side of the qasun, away, presumably, from anyone who might overhear her screaming.

But before she could scream herself hoarse demanding to be let go, put down, she was lowered to the ground again, though the arms didn't release her.

"Ember," Felix whispered, so softly that the only reason she could hear him at all was because he spoke directly into her ear. "It's okay. Calm down."

She sucked in a breath. It caught in her throat on the way in and wrenched its way out as a sob.

Felix's iron grip on her arms loosened from restraint to embrace. "Shh. It's okay."

But it wasn't. Eli was a dirty traitor and her father thought she was useless.

And that was the point, wasn't it? She was useless. The Spindle hadn't even been there at the southwestern wall this evening, and nothing she did brought it.

No wonder Eli preferred the Brothers. At least they fed and clothed and healed him. She had never been able to do any of that. Not in Dusk, where more often than not, it was Eli working to help keep her alive. Not in Frost, where she'd allowed the queen to get her hooks in him, and then he'd taken a knife between the ribs because she couldn't convince the queen of the truth of what she was trying to say. And now, not in Sand, where it was the Brothers who'd patched up his wounds, anointed him with perfume, fed the gauntness out of his face.

Felix turned Ember toward him, and she sobbed painful, tearless sobs against his shoulder. His hand moved in gentle circles up and down her back. "Shh, shh. It's okay."

And then, as if he could read her thoughts, or maybe she was speaking them aloud, she honestly didn't know, he continued. "You're not useless."

"I am. Can't even … the bloody Spindle…"

He pulled back, and though she immediately missed the warmth of him, the steady in and out of his breaths against her cheek, Ember didn't protest.

Maybe it was right that Felix leave. She trusted him, too, and that meant he could betray her just as much as Eli could.

And that, she thought, was something she wasn't sure she'd be able to take. Eli, she could survive. Her father, she could survive. But Felix?

It was absurd, she knew that even as she was considering it. She'd only known Felix for some weeks — how could the idea of him turning coat on her feel like it would break her in ways she wasn't even broken up by Eli?

But it would, and she knew it.

Maybe it was better if he left her, stepped back, disappeared from her life, now, before he could hurt her like that.

That thought hurt almost as bad as the possibility of betrayal.

"Ember, look at me."

She didn't want to. It was safe with her face turned down at her feet, where neither of them had to face the reality of her thoughts, the shame of her actions.

But she deserved it, whatever Felix was about to say. She deserved to hear it, and she should face it, prove to him, at least, that she wasn't a complete coward, even if that wasn't entirely true.

She bit down the rest of her sobs, swallowed hard to make them stop tearing up her breaths, and looked up.

He looked steadily back, a frown creasing his forehead but his eyes soft. Not angry — worried. He rested his hands on her shoulders, and the touch was grounding, something other than her own impossible swirl of thoughts to focus on. He stared into her eyes and spoke low and gentle. "You're not useless."

Ember kissed him.

Felix went deathly still at the touch, not even breathing, and she understood a moment too late that she shouldn't act on her impulses. Sand filled her head with confusion, with restless, stupid ideas, and she couldn't keep acting on her impulses if she wanted to ever have friends again.

Heat flooded her face, her head, her body — she was sure that even her arms were blushing with the sudden sick of embarrassment. She started to pull away, to stammer out an apology, a desperate plea that he forgive her and forget this had ever happened, but just then, Felix made a sound and relaxed. "Stay," he whispered into the hair's breadth of space she'd managed between them and pulled her back in again.

Ember echoed that little noise, found as it slipped out of her that it was almost a whimper. This time, when their mouths touched, Felix kissed her back. He slid his hands up from her shoulders to the back of her neck and held her there, his fingers stroking slowly at the soft hairs at her nape.

His lips were as soft and warm as the rest of him, with the same kind of unexpected iron strength beneath it. There was power in gentleness — Ember felt foolish for never noticing that before. Because Felix was gentle, everything about him warm and soft and considerate, but that didn't make him weak. It made him *kind*.

She loved that kindness, that considerateness, that warmth. She'd grown up in a world that considered kindness, softness, an opportunity to take advantage, and she hadn't known until Felix that those were the things she yearned for most.

She loved him.

The thought struck her across the face and chest, as hard as a slap but without the pain. She pulled back suddenly, desperate for air, and looked at him. She was close enough that even in the dark, she could make out the light dusting of freckles across his nose, that lovely blue-gray color of his eyes. He was watching her, a dazed little smile on his lips. A couple of curls had fallen onto his forehead — Ember finally, finally, summoned the courage to brush them back.

His hair was surprisingly cool to the touch, even in the heat of the desert night, even despite the fire-warm red that had always intrigued her. She brushed back those curls, then found that she didn't want to stop touching his hair.

She should say something. She wanted to say something. Something about how she loved his hair, his eyes, his freckles, the warmth of his fingers or the goodness of his heart. Something that would add to the moment, something that would make him melt inside the way he made her do. But when she opened her mouth, nothing came out.

Felix smiled. "It's okay. Now be quiet and kiss me."

Ember didn't need to be asked twice.

There was force in her kiss now, pressure and intention that hadn't been there before. Maybe she couldn't say all the things she wanted to — maybe they all got tangled up in her throat before they made it out of her mouth — but she could still make herself understood.

Felix responded in kind, his fingers tightening in her hair, his shoulders leaning in so they were matching force for force. Ember's lips tingled from the pressure, but that only heightened the sensation, added to the heat stirring inside her.

She caught her fingers in the back of his head, a

couple of them wrapped up in curls like even his hair wanted her to stay where she was. She pressed them in, seeking the warmth of skin beneath the cool of hair.

There was a very faint noise, a soft sort of click, unfamiliar and strangely mechanical, and suddenly, it was as if every bone and muscle in Felix's body gave out at once. His fingers and arms went slack, his head and shoulders sagged. For a moment, he leaned against Ember, caught in their embrace, and then he slid like liquid through her arms and crumpled to the ground.

Ember stared down at him. His eyes, which a moment ago had been lit up with happiness and desire, were now fixed blankly on nothing.

She opened her mouth again, probably to say something, to ask uselessly what was wrong, what had she done, but those words, too, tangled up in her throat and refused to fall.

Ember knew that look. She'd seen it so many times in her workshop in Frost that she'd never be able to forget it.

That was how every deactivated doll looked when she'd turned off their power.

Ember screamed.

Chapter Thirteen

EMBER SCREAMED and screamed and screamed, until she was sure that her voice would give out and her throat would crack from the strain, but it didn't help. Even screaming didn't let out the strange horror she was feeling.

Felix was a doll.

She backed away from him — from it — her screams morphing back into the forgotten sobs of a few minutes before.

The doll didn't move. Didn't stand and smile and say that this was all some kind of cruel joke. Of course not. She'd turned it off — there was no power running through the clockwork and programming that made dolls function.

Noises other than her screaming sobs filled the space. Footsteps. Quick, half-panicked male voices. She recognized them. She fought to identify them.

Shahif put a hand on Ember's shoulder, blocking her stumbling backwards steps. "Ember? What is it? What's happened?"

Ember pointed at the powered-off doll. Her finger, her arm, her whole body, was shaking. "He's ... he's..."

She couldn't say it. Saying it would make it real.

Shahif frowned a little as he glanced at the doll, but he didn't seem surprised. Not shocked or horrified or confused. Not any of the things he ought to feel finding out something like that. "Yes," he agreed, a simple statement of unremarkable fact.

Had he known already? How was that possible?

Why would someone keep that from her?

Another man, slower than Shahif, came up to them now, knelt down in front of the doll, reached hands for his — its — head. For a moment, Ember had the wild urge to knock the man aside, protect Felix from any meddling hands, as if everyone in Sand were an enemy trying to hurt them.

But then the other man turned around. It was Papa, and the urge to shove him away died.

Papa scowled at her. His voice came out as a snap. "Be quiet, child."

Ember snapped her mouth shut, cutting off the next scream mid-breath, but she couldn't stop the tears — those continued to fall, hard and hot. She pressed her palm to her mouth to at least muffle the sound, keep herself from accidentally screaming again.

Papa turned back to Felix, the line of his shoulders tight like he had more to say and was choosing to ignore it. He brushes his fingers along the back of Felix's head, and Ember thought she heard that same mechanical little click as before, and Felix sat up.

But it wasn't Felix anymore. Not the kind, curious Frost boy she loved. This doll was a mask of Felix, wearing his face, his body, but everything that made him who he was, the person Ember had kissed just minutes ago, was gone.

Ember hadn't known Felix was a doll. She'd never considered the possibility, at least partly because he didn't act like a doll. He didn't wear that impossibly large smile like a piece of clothing. Didn't move in that same too-precise way that made every other doll she'd seen look just a little bit wrong. Dolls weren't curious or thoughtful. Didn't ask questions or disobey orders. They'd been going mad in Frost, yes, but that had been under the orders of their developer. The prince of Sand.

Papa.

Felix wasn't like that. He had thoughts. Opinions. A freedom of will and movement like any other person.

He'd asked Ember to kiss him.

And now, he sat perfectly still in front of Papa, smiling too wide at nothing, his eyes unfocused and blank. Unmistakably a doll.

Ember clenched her teeth and swallowed down the sick that rose in her throat.

Papa turned back to her and stood, still scowling. "What did you do?"

"Me?" Ember had to struggle to keep her voice from becoming another scream. "I didn't do anything!"

"No? What do you call this, then?" He jerked a thumb back toward Felix, who was standing up now, brushing the sand off his clothes and still looking at nothing.

"He's a … a doll."

The words burned on the way out. She forced them through her teeth anyway.

"My *best* doll," Papa corrected, as if that should be obvious. "And you've ruined him!"

She looked at Felix. He stood perfectly still, smiling hugely, waiting for his next order. "Felix?"

He glanced at her, smiled a little wider, bobbed his head once in acknowledgment. Didn't move toward her. Didn't speak. Didn't reach for her hand and tell her it was going to be all right.

Had she done that? She'd never seen a doll reactivated after turning it off, had only been in charge of stopping them from ranting about Frost's southern wall, which, for all the queen tried to cover it up, was indeed cracking.

She didn't know what happened to those dolls afterward. What they were like when they were turned back on.

"Reset to basics," Papa growled, his voice tight as it came out through his teeth. "Do you know how much work it took to get this one programmed to that Vallenovich man's specifications? How many times I had to scrap and rewrite him entirely? And now you've gone and wiped it all! The programming, the work, the years of development — gone! What. Did. You. Do?"

The last words, barely strung together into a coherent question, burned hotter than direct rays of Sand sunlight.

Ember hadn't really stopped crying, maybe not even from the moment she started somewhere in the middle of tearing into Eli, but now the tears redoubled. She wiped at them, embarrassed to be crying so hard in front of Papa — and over a doll, of all things! — but unable to stop. "I didn't mean to."

She hadn't. She hadn't even known something like this was a possibility. That she might be able to reach around, slide fingers through his hair, and turn him off. She'd thought he was a person, and people didn't have power buttons at the tops of their spines.

Papa's scowl deepened, unimpressed. "Obviously."

"It was ... I..." She reached behind her own head to indicate the place. "It was an accident."

"And what were you doing jamming fingers at my doll's power cell?"

No. That wasn't his information to demand, his memory to have. Their kiss was hers, hers and the boy she loved, and not for Papa to know about.

"Mikail," Shahif said. He spoke softly, just loud enough to hear, as if unsure of his welcome. Ember had almost forgotten he was there, would've forgotten entirely if his hand had come off her shoulder. But it hadn't, and he'd kept the same gentle, grounding pressure on her as he had after her first storm. Not enough to interrupt, and certainly not enough to calm, but there just the same. "It's been a long day — perhaps we should get some rest and come back to this tomorrow."

Papa grunted, but a little bit of the tension in his shoulders loosened, and, after a quiet moment, he nodded. "Don't think we're done here, girl," he mumbled at Ember as he started back toward the qasun. "I still have questions for you."

He glanced back at Felix, jerked his head in the direction of his going. "You're coming, too, doll."

Felix hurried to catch up.

Ember watched them until they had turned the corner toward the qasun door, swallowing hard the whole time to keep down the sobs and screams and sick that kept churning inside her.

The desert seemed a little emptier, a little colder, now.

Shahif patted her shoulder. "Come. You need some rest."

Ember didn't see how that would help anything, but she was in no state to argue. Shahif had been right about most things so far — it was probably foolish not to believe him now.

She let herself be led into the qasun. The woman of cloth who'd been looking after her was waiting just inside the door; Shahif handed Ember off to her.

She could feel the woman's gaze on her face as they made their way back to her room. She couldn't make out her eyes, her face, behind the veil, but there was an unmistakable heaviness at her temple, that skin-crawling sensation of being watched, that told her the woman was looking at her anyway.

Ember didn't say anything, walked in silence half a step in front of the woman and didn't try to engage her at all. There was no point to it — women of cloth didn't, or couldn't, talk. Still, she did yank harder at her control, forced herself to not feel the tears still clawing at her eyes, focused instead on trying to think through her next move.

Felix was a doll. That much was certain. He was a doll, and always had been.

But it wasn't until Ember turned him off that he really *became* a doll. Before then, he'd been a person just as much as she was. How much of that was programming, set into his clockwork and electrics at his building, she didn't know.

How much did it matter? And what did it mean about how she felt?

That was the knot she wasn't ready to untangle.

They reached her room then, and Ember couldn't remember a time when she was so grateful for a chance to be alone, locked up somewhere where no one could see or hear her, where she was mostly left to herself. She dropped onto the couch nearly as quickly and bonelessly as a powered-off doll herself.

The cushions were soft beneath her tired body, the fabric smooth and pleasant against her overheated skin. She ran her fingers across the cushions, enjoying the sensation, thinking of nothing but the gentle bumps of the fabric grain, the lightly furry, manufactured feel of it. Rubbing away the memory of Felix's hair under her fingertips, his lips, warm and soft and enthusiastic, on hers…

No.

Ember buried her face into the cushion, pressing hard enough to make breathing difficult. This was nothing like that, nothing at all, and she wouldn't think about it ever again.

It was nothing. Meant nothing. She'd been mistaken about Felix this whole time. He'd kept a secret from her — the biggest secret he could possibly keep — and that made him untrustable. Untrustable, and therefore unloveable.

Maybe it wasn't Eli who'd betrayed her. Maybe it was Felix, and she hadn't wanted to see it because she didn't want to believe it.

A fresh round of tears threatened to drown her. She jammed her face harder into the cushion, but that didn't prevent them from coming, only stopped her noises from carrying.

In all the nonsense from the last few minutes, she'd almost disregarded the nonsense that began it. Those moments outside the qasun with a doll she thought she loved had started because she'd gone to the 'akhelum and smacked Eli around for something he maybe hadn't even done.

Eli said he didn't do it. She'd refused to listen because that left only the possibility that Felix was the one who had — a possibility too horrible to consider. Or, at least, it had been when she first had to consider it.

Now, it seemed like the obvious answer.

Felix was a doll, controlled by doll programming, obeying the orders from his developer. He could've sent every moment, every word, every soft brush of fingers and stupid, besotted look Ember had given him straight back to anyone who wanted to look.

Maybe Papa had seen it all.

Or maybe it had gone straight to the Brothers. To the doll division of Envoys, headed by Vallenovich.

Maybe the queen of Frost herself was watching her still.

This thought, even more than any other, turned Ember's stomach with fear and revulsion. She thought she'd escaped Frost, escaped the queen. Ember didn't know everything there was to know about how dolls operated, but she was perfectly well aware that the Frost dolls reported back to the queen in some way. It was how she had her people tailed, monitored, and controlled. Why there were questions people couldn't ask and places they couldn't go.

And Felix was a Frost doll. Papa might have built him, but he built him to go to Frost. To be claimed as the son of the head of the queen's doll division. Whatever else might've been happening inside his programs, Felix was meant to be a Frost doll.

Ember shuddered, and the cold of it ran deeper than her skin, into her blood and bones. She'd always thought their meeting a coincidence, just one of those things that happened sometimes. Felix had been a friendly stranger curious about the obvious outworlder in the crowd. A new face in a sea of his usual way of life. He'd said hello and offered her an apple because he was just that sort of person.

But maybe it wasn't a coincidence. Maybe he'd been sent, by Vallenovich or the queen. Ordered to be friendly, gain Ember's trust, and report everything right back to them. Maybe he'd been a plant. A spy. A tailing doll much more clever than the usual tails that followed people around Frost.

Ember had never really questioned why Felix was so good at spotting and getting rid of their tails. He'd said something about being used to it, having years of practice dodging them or losing them in crowds, and she'd accepted that as something that was just true about him. He was cleverer than the dolls, or knew something from being

Vallenovich's son that made him able to escape their notice.

But maybe he was just sending them messages to bugger off because he was a better tail than they could ever be. Maybe all the dolls were in it together — one would follow Ember around that Felix could help her dodge so that she would think he was on her side. So that she would trust him and not wonder for a moment if he had some other mission, some other purpose rather than just liking her and wanting to see what was past the southern wall.

Maybe everything, from the apple to the kiss, had been a ruse meant to trap her, break her, render her the useless, blubbering puddle she was now, so the queen could get whatever it was she was after.

And, maybe worse, Ember wasn't sure if she even cared.

Or, rather, she did definitely *care* — of course she did, she'd hardly be this useless, blubbering puddle if she didn't — but she wasn't sure she could change it. Everything inside her hurt, hurt worse than she'd ever hurt before, and she didn't have the strength of either muscle or will to stop hurting, clean off her tears, and get off the couch.

She'd never considered herself the sort of person who gave up, who succumbed to difficulty of getting through it, whatever "it" happened to be. Dusk built people strong, and stubborn, and sometimes too much of each for their own good. Only those people too stubborn to die survived inside the cold and dark, the dwindling rations of food and light and hope passed around behind the walls, and she'd always thought herself to be one of those sorts of people, too. Alive because she was too stubborn to give up.

Maybe, and she was horrified to find this thought inside her own head, maybe it was just because she'd never been hurt badly enough. For as dreary as Dusk could be, as dark and hopeless the stretch of her life was doomed for, the dry, consuming pain of hopelessness was better tempered by the fact that she was capable of doing something about it.

What she could do, tinkering with her compass and some of old Korrah's artifacts from Before, dreaming of what the world had been like in those times, retelling Korrah's stories or the things she read or imagined from her father's old books — it hadn't been much, but at least it was something to do. Something that made the darkness bearable, the hopelessness a little lighter.

At least there she'd had a friend.

Ember wept into the couch cushion until her eyes were gritty and dry and too heavy to hold open anymore.

Chapter Fourteen

EMBER HAD NEVER HAD A LONGER-SEEMING night. Given that, especially in the dead of winter, Dusk never brightened beyond a twilight glow so that midnight was barely any darker than midday, she figured that was a pretty meaningful statement.

This night seemed endless, and she'd grown up where night was almost literally endless.

Truthfully, she wasn't even sure when she first woke up if it was the same day at all. She'd been storm-addled for three days before, and even that was less confusing than waking up with her face smashed against a damp couch cushion, her head and neck throbbing with every heartbeat, her insides twisting and aching like she was about to be sick. Her chest felt like it had been scooped clean, leaving nothing but a dull, hollow thudding inside her, a hammer smashing against her breastbone in a counterpoint to the headache and muscle kinks.

She rolled over, propped herself up to sitting, rubbed her fingers across her head and neck, seeking out and trying to massage away the worst of the pain. Her hair swung loose and damp in front of her eyes, and sweat trickled from her temple into her ear. The room was stifling hot and as dark as eyes closed, and she wasn't even sure what she was doing here, why her eyelids felt like sand when they moved over her eyeballs.

She'd been having a dream. Something terrible, frightening. Something about losing control, of herself, of the situation around her, of the people she loved. She'd been standing somewhere empty and strange, helpless in the face of destruction.

But she couldn't remember what it was, what the destruction had been, why she was powerless to change it, and that was just as terrible as the powerlessness itself. She was afraid, and she didn't even know why.

"Just a dream," she whispered, out loud so the words would hit her ears and mean what they said. "It wasn't real. I was dreaming."

But, if she wasn't dreaming anymore, why did those feelings persist now, into the real, physical, not-dream world?

She pushed her hair out of her eyes, ran her fingers through it, focused on the sharp little sensation of her nails against her scalp. That was real. It felt nice. Soothing, the way it should feel to scratch at something that was not quite yet an itch, but that was about to become one. Her nails weren't long or sharp enough to hurt, but they left a tingling little trail in their wake just the same.

"Just a dream," she repeated, a little louder this time. She'd make herself believe it, even if she had to shout the words so the whole qasun could hear. "I'm in Sand. In my room where the storms can't touch me. Where dreams mean nothing. I'm fine. Everything's fine."

She wasn't sure if she believed that — she spoke it aloud, willed herself to believe it anyway.

She wanted to go back to sleep. Wanted to sleep off the headache, the cramps, the hollow banging in her chest. It had been a long day, and she wanted it to be over. But now that she was awake, her eyes felt wide open, her limbs full of that same jittery energy they'd had nearly every moment since she'd come here.

Ember breathed, long and slow, forcing the air deep into her lungs as if to prove to that hollow feeling that she still had lungs. Even breathing deeply felt strange, like she'd spent the last hours gasping for air and not getting enough.

Which was what she'd been doing, hadn't she?

The full memory of what happened came back to her like a blow. Not that she'd actually forgotten it, but like she'd forgotten how her mind and body had reacted, forgotten why she wasn't breathing right or thinking straight. It all hit her with blunt, all-over force, a club rather than a knife, and she slumped back down onto the couch.

Her eyes were dry this time, her screams used up. She stared at nothing and let it all wash over her — Eli and Felix, Papa and the Brothers, Sand and Frost and Dusk, the Spindle and the Leshii and Before.

Maybe, just maybe, if she lay very still, it would bury her.

Her eyes slipped closed, and she fell back into the darkness.

THE NEXT TIME SHE WOKE, it was to the touch of clothed fingers on her shoulder. It was still dark, but the courtyard beyond her room hummed with early-morning activity.

Dolls, most of them. Would Felix be among them now?

Ember shivered and shoved that thought aside.

The woman of cloth was bending over her, invisible

eyes fixed on her face. Ember didn't look back — she already knew she wouldn't be able to find the woman's face beneath the veil, and she was done trying to do impossible things.

She'd spent a long time assuming that impossible things were only those things that others were too afraid to try. That was the mind of a scientist, after all — the desire to understand was embedded into her nature.

But maybe some things were best left unquestioned. Maybe there was some merit to those people who claimed that ignorance was bliss.

Eli had always tried to tell her that she'd be better off if she didn't think of the world as a mystery she had to unravel, and she'd spent most of her life determined to prove him wrong. But maybe he was right. Maybe there were some mysteries best left unsolved. Maybe sometimes the walls were there for a reason, to keep some things out that didn't need to be let in.

It couldn't hurt to try, could it? That was something else scientists did — they tried things. Lots of those things didn't work, and to a good scientist, the things that didn't work were just as valuable as the things that did.

She'd tried unraveling every mystery, and that had led her here. Maybe she could try letting things go instead — maybe that would make her happier.

After all, it couldn't make her less happy than she was now.

The woman of cloth shook Ember's shoulder again, with a little more insistence than she'd had before. Ember flicked her off but did also look up at her to prove she was awake.

There was a pause, a moment that felt heavy with sudden expectation, and then the woman of cloth spoke, softly, through her veil. "Ember."

Ember shot upright, her reluctance to move overcome by her surprise. Women of cloth didn't speak. Whether that was because they chose not to or because they couldn't, she wasn't clear, but Shahif had said they didn't speak, and every encounter she'd had with one, including this one, made that clear.

She'd even asked this woman if she could talk, and the woman had indicated not. She remember that, because it was the moment she'd realized that trying to draw out the woman of cloth was a waste.

"You—"

"Shh. Keep your voice down. I can't be found out," she interrupted, and the woman's imperious tone, the soft accent, was something Ember thought she knew.

She frowned at the woman. "Who are you?"

"Shh!"

Fine. She could play a little. Ember lowered her voice obligingly. "Who are you?"

The woman lifted her veil, and for a moment, Ember stared up at her face without recognition. Perhaps that wasn't strange — the last time she'd seen that face, it had been in an entirely different place and context, and Sand had changed it. Gone were the painted blue eyelids and lips; now her pale skin looked sunburnt and dry. Against the washed-out blues of her palace, she'd looked almost like she'd been born of the ice walls, as cold and hard and beautiful as the palace itself. Against the walls of the qasun, wrapped entirely up in cloth, she seemed almost normal — human in a way she'd never looked in Frost.

Ember jumped to her feet, surprise and fear building in equal measure in her. Her voice was a hiss. "You. How did you find me?"

The queen of Frost removed her veil and the headwrap that held it on, loosing the dark hair that Ember had never seen so undone, so tangled. "You are not the only person with a copter. I knew where you were going."

Ember's thoughts flashed to Felix, and the fear that he'd been reporting back to the queen this whole time rose once again.

But she wasn't going to mention Felix to the queen. Wasn't going to let her know anything if she didn't already know it. "How?"

The queen smiled, and that was an expression Ember definitely recognized, that malicious little smirk she gave. "You're not subtle, *devushka*."

"Don't call me that. I'm not your child."

She very nearly screamed right then and there, loud and long until she'd attracted someone's attention — maybe Shahif's, maybe even Papa's. It almost didn't matter.

The queen of Frost had followed her to Sand, had been in her room, seeing and hearing who knew what as Ember tried to find the Spindle, get to the Leshii, help her father fix this broken world.

She didn't scream, but it was close. First, though, she wanted answers.

"What are you doing here?"

"About the same thing as you — looking for something."

"What?"

The queen considered her for a moment, and Ember knew that look, too — she was considering how much she ought to say, how to lie and manipulate most gracefully, so that her listener wouldn't think at all that's what she was doing.

Well, Ember was through falling for it. She crossed her arms and stared right back, daring the queen to try.

"Blueprints," she said at last, with enough sincerity to

her voice that Ember didn't think she was actually lying. Probably hedging, preparing to turn her answers toward manipulation, but not lying yet.

"Blueprints?" Ember repeated. She knew the word only vaguely, had heard it tossed off once or twice, maybe read it in one of Papa's old books from Before. It was something about building plans, she thought, but she didn't actually know what the word meant. "What kind of blueprints?"

The queen smiled again, that same small, brittle thing that had always set Ember's teeth on edge. "Are you offering to help me, little scientist?"

"I'm not a scientist. I told you that."

"And yet, here you are."

"What's that mean?"

"What do you think it means?"

"I'm in no mood for games."

"Obviously." The queen's smile stilled, and her expression grew serious again. "Ember, come back to Frost with me."

Ember blinked. There were a dozen different things she'd expected to hear from the queen of Frost, but that was not one of them. "What?"

"I have a copter coming for me in two days. You can be on it, too."

"I'm not going anywhere with you."

"Ember." She'd never seen the queen so determined, so worried, not even when she was begging Ember to fix her unbroken machines. "What your father's doing — it's dangerous. It's going to destroy everything all over again. The walls protected Frost then from total disaster. It can do it again. We have the resources to last, and with Mikail's blueprints, we can fix our dolls, fix our walls. We can keep him out."

Ember scowled back, unmoved. The queen would say anything to get her way, and to hear her speak ill of her father, even obliquely? She'd laugh if she had mind to. As if the queen of Frost, of all the controlling, manipulative people, had the right to feel superior in any way to Papa. It was absurd.

This was absurd.

"What happens if someone else finds out you're here?"

The queen's lips twitched, and fear flashed through her eyes. She tried to quell it, smiling her cold smile and flicking her hair over her shoulder. "Nothing good, I'm sure," she said coolly, but Ember had already seen it, that fear her conscious actions weren't able to hide.

The queen was afraid. Of Papa? Of Sand?

It didn't matter — Ember already knew her next move.

She grabbed the queen, turning her around so she held the queen's arm twisted behind her back like that one Brother had caught her, pulling her arm around until she heard the queen suck in a pained breath. "What—"

"You picked the wrong person to try and appeal to," Ember whispered in her ear. "I'm not falling for your lies again."

"I'm not—"

Ember jerked at the queen's arm hard enough to shut her up. "Walk, or I'll get a doll in here to drag you. They might be yours in Frost, but here in Sand, they answer only to the prince."

That was an assumption on Ember's part, but an assumption she was comfortable making just the same. She didn't, not even a little bit, think of Felix scrambling to catch up with her father and ignoring Ember in his — its — rush to do as it was told.

The queen huffed, but she walked, out of the room and into the hall. "This won't make your father love you."

If Ember had a knife in her hand, she would've used it then, swiping at the queen's back, or maybe sticking it between her ribs the way she'd had her Envoy do to Eli to prove she was serious.

But she hadn't actually seen her knife since coming to Sand. She'd had it in her hand when Shahif came to fetch them from the copter, but it went missing after that. Confiscated, probably — if the qasun were hers, she wouldn't want it full of armed strangers with unknown motives, either.

She walked the queen forward with just the twist of her arms. The queen whimpered protests.

"You don't know what you're doing," she said, her voice low enough not to echo as they crossed the courtyard, still mostly empty in the dawn gray. Only a few dolls fiddled with a couple of the courtyard stands, smiles wide and fingers precise in ways no person could ever achieve.

Ember didn't look at their faces, wasn't sure what she'd do if Felix turned up among them. Didn't want to find that out in front of the queen of Frost, who was, right now, doing some top-tier begging.

"Please, please. This is a bad idea. He's not who you think he is, he's not safe."

They made it through the courtyard without attracting any attention — the dolls had their jobs and weren't usually very distractable anyway.

Away from the dolls, Ember relaxed. Just a little — just enough to hear the words the queen was saying.

Not who you think he is.

"Oh?" she answered. "So the prince of Sand is *not* my father? Who is he, then? A doll?"

She spoke the words sarcastically, aiming for a taunt, but the idea hit her with a brutality she wasn't expecting.

Felix was a doll. Had been this whole time, and Ember

didn't even know it, didn't even consider it as a possibility because he didn't present like other dolls. Was it possible that other people were, too? Was Papa?

She shivered away from that idea. It wasn't so — she'd known Papa too long, too well, for him to hide something like that. As strange as it was to realize, she'd only known Felix a few weeks, and she had no idea of him before coming to Frost.

Papa had raised her, and no doll, no matter how well-made, would survive long in Dusk. There'd be no one there to repair its clockwork, maintain its programming.

Papa was a person. He was her father.

"That's not … Ember, please, you have to listen to me…"

But listening to the queen of Frost had only brought her lies and grief. She kept walking them forward.

"He won't protect you. I can."

"Protect me?" Ember laughed, a hard single syllable that didn't sound like anything that had come from her mouth before. "How? By locking me up behind a wall? Lying to me about why those walls are there? Brain-washing people into believing you're Mother Atalanta come back to save the world again?"

They were at Papa's door. It was closed. Ember knocked.

The queen tried once more before it opened. "He won't like seeing me here."

No, Ember imagined not. That was the very point of this.

She'd found the bloody queen of Frost lurking around Papa's home. If anything would make him forgive her for her failures, it would be finding an enemy lurking around inside their walls.

The door opened. Papa scowled. "What now, child?"

The words were barely out of his mouth when his eyes fell on the queen in Ember's grip. The queen straightened, as if she hadn't been begging just a second ago. Her voice turned once again to ice. "Mikail."

"Natalya," he answered. His own voice shook.

Chapter Fifteen

PAPA OPENED HIS DOOR, waved both Ember and the queen inside. He closed it, turned the lock, then lit a couple of lanterns.

His room was lush, with carpets covering the floors and art hung all over the walls. His windows, too, looked out over the courtyard, but they were large and many so he had more than a single small view of what was happening in the busiest part of the qasun. He had a sleeping couch and softly upholstered chairs, pillows and blankets piled up on every one of them, and even an upright wooden chest of drawers to keep things in.

He gestured for the queen and Ember to sit. The queen did, her spine straight, her fingers folded on her lap.

Ember elected to stand. She let go of the queen so she could sit down, but she wasn't about to step away, give this woman any chance of escaping.

"How'd you get in here?" Papa asked at last. He, too, remained standing, in front of the queen, looking down at her so she was sandwiched between him and Ember.

The queen fluttered inside her costume. "You keep an

entire class of people under total wraps. You ought to know better than that, Mikail."

"'Sir' will do from you."

"Honestly." The queen tinkled a laugh. "You really think you're worth that kind of respect?"

"I hear you call yourself a queen."

"I *am* a queen."

Papa scoffed. "You're more of a pretender than I've ever been." He sobered. "Why are you here?"

"For the same reason I've always done everything: to find a way to protect my city from your ideas."

Ember wasn't holding onto the queen anymore, but her fingers curled warningly tight against the back of the chair where she sat. Papa wanted to fix the world. If that was dangerous, it was because it meant Frost wouldn't need to contain its people inside its walls. It meant that the world beyond Frost wouldn't be either endless desert or endless tundra.

If the world was better, the people of Frost wouldn't need their walls. And that would mean they wouldn't need their queen to maintain the walls, or the lies she told about them.

She wasn't interested in protecting Frost for the sake of its people — she was only interested in keeping it isolated, unaware of the world beyond it, so that she could keep her grip on those people. She only wanted to protect herself, her own power.

Papa seemed to understand the same thing from those words — he scoffed again and leaned in close to the queen's face, pushing her back into the chair. "Don't toy with me, Natalya. We both know what you really want. The only thing you've ever wanted."

"And what's that?" Her voice had gone faint under Papa's closeness, his stare. Ember bit her lip to keep from grinning.

"Power," Papa whispered. He pulled back a bit, smiled a chilly Frost smile. "You've come to the wrong place, Natta. You'll find that Sand answers to me."

He turned away, but only for a moment; when he spun back around, he was holding some kind of device Ember hadn't seen before, a bulky metal box balanced on one hand and forearm while his other hand pressed a series of buttons at the top.

A moment later, there was a knock on the door.

"Your Highness," said the doll on the other side. It inclined its head and stepped into the room in response to a couple more buttons.

"I want our guest here confined to a woman's quarters. We will need round-the-clock guard. Armed, please."

Something inside the doll whirred for a moment, then the synthetic skin of its left hand split down the middle, and the fingers turned back. In place of a hand, it now had a knife.

It pointed the knife at the queen's throat. "Stand up."

The queen obeyed — she couldn't do otherwise, not with the tip of the doll's knife at the delicate skin of her throat.

"Walk."

The doll didn't even need to put its hand on her. The queen kept her chin high, probably to keep it from bumping the knife, which the doll was able to hold without wavering to the same threatening place against her neck.

They walked out of the room. The doll closed the door behind them.

Ember let out a breath, aware only as the queen left that she hadn't been breathing quite right while she was there. Then she turned to Papa and smiled. "I found her.

She said she wanted some blueprints, and that she has a copter coming for her in two days."

Papa was still typing into his box and didn't look up at Ember's words.

She edged a little closer, curious about the device. It was something she hadn't seen before, and judging by the way a doll had responded to it, she thought it was maybe for the dolls. Something to give them orders or alter bits of their programming.

Maybe it was the device that showed up in Frost's logs as "unknown developer."

Frost was almost a day's flight away from here — the idea of a little metal box capable of sending a signal that far was extraordinary. She wondered what it would look like on the inside, what sort of gears and wires she'd find. If she could look at it, trace all those internal bits, and figure out how it worked, maybe even how to improve it. Boost its signal, or reduce the number of buttons that needed to be pushed, because Papa was still typing on it.

The arm holding it was getting strained — the box was obviously heavy. Maybe it didn't need to be that heavy. Maybe there was a way to cut down on the weight—

"What're you staring at?"

His voice interrupted the ideas rushing through Ember's thoughts. She flinched at the sharpness in his tone but hopefully he didn't see that. She smiled instead. "Is that for doll programming?"

Papa grunted. "It's one of them."

"Are there more?"

He looked at her like he'd never heard a stupider question. Ember's face ran suddenly hot, and she dropped her gaze. "So. The queen of Frost."

It wasn't a graceful change of subject, but it was clear

that Papa didn't want her to talk about his programming box, and that was the first other thing in her brain.

Papa grunted again.

"I caught her in my room. She wanted me to go with her back to Frost. I said no, obviously."

"Obviously, or you wouldn't be bothering me now."

Ember's face got somehow hotter. "I … wasn't trying to bother you."

"And yet, here you still are."

She wouldn't cry. Surely she was out of tears by now, after the painful amount of weeping she'd done into her couch cushion. But somehow, they still came, that hot throb of tears that ached behind her eyes. She cleared her throat quietly and refused to let them fall. "What are you going to do with her?"

He looked up from his device at last, but only so he could glare at Ember, clearly annoyed by the question. "Why are you still here?"

Ember dropped her eyes, fighting hard against the tears, determined not to cry. She didn't trust her voice to not crack, so she didn't dare answer, either.

Papa let out a breath, his shoulders relaxing a tiny bit from being pulled up tight close to his ears. "You want to help? Don't spend your time worrying about dolls and the politics of other places. I need you to find the Spindle. That's all."

Ember nodded with renewed determination. She'd lost a bit of her way, taken her eyes off the mission she had, spent too much time thinking about dolls and love and the queen of Frost.

But she did have a mission. A thing she was here to do. She wouldn't be distracted again.

. . .

SHE STAYED IN HER ROOM, napping on and off for most of the day, and no one bothered her. She needed to get inside the 'akhelum, needed to get to the Spindle, but she couldn't think straight with exhaustion clogging up her mind and limbs as it was.

In between her naps, she stayed lying on her couch, listening to the muffled noises outside of her window. People talking, sometimes understandable, but mostly either in voices too quiet to hear or understand.

Once, she peeked out at them.

Dolls.

The courtyard was always mostly dolls, always outnumbering people three or four to one. But as she scanned the courtyard today, noting the way the busyness of it broke down, she realized that there wasn't a single real person out there. Not one. The whole space was filled with dolls, and they were all doing their own things, but there was an eerie synchrony to their movements anyway.

One doll was straightening a table, and its neighbor was walking through the offerings of the courtyard, but even though their actions were different, their limbs moved together — each step of the wandering doll matched with each item the straightening doll turned.

And that same perfectly matched timing was shared across the whole courtyard, through every doll doing anything at all that could be synchronized.

Ember shivered away from the sight and didn't look out the window again.

Eventually, the rest started doing some good, and when she woke up from maybe the third or fourth bout of anxious dreams, she found it easier than before to keep her eyes open, to make straight lines with her thoughts.

The courtyard had quieted, and judging by the brightness coming through her window, she guessed it was somewhere around midday. Not a great time to leave the qasun, but she'd already wasted the whole morning trying to get some rest, and she wasn't keen to waste more.

She grabbed her compass and sandals, slid both of them onto their proper spots, and left her room. Without a woman of cloth guarding her door, she didn't even have to slip by anyone in order to leave, and she sent a quick thought of gratitude toward Papa for that.

The dolls in the courtyard all turned to watch her as she hurried through the space. Ember fixed her gaze on the far hall where she was headed and didn't meet any of their eyes.

It was indeed midday, or close to it — the sun was almost directly overhead as she slipped out of the qasun, her shadow a formless splotch at her feet as she hurried across the sand toward the 'akhelum. The heat pressed down on her head and shoulders, threatened her legs with buckling and her lungs with burning, but she set her jaw and ignored it.

The 'akhelum tugged at her attention, urging her toward it, begging her to return to her post at the southwestern wall, and go mad with the fact that she couldn't get through it, but she ignored that, too.

She wasn't going to the 'akhelum, not right now. Not like this. First, she needed a way to hide herself. And the queen had pointed out one very effective way of doing so.

You have a whole class of people you keep completely under wraps.

Ember could almost hear the words that had sparked the beginning of the idea. She'd resented them at first, used as they were by the queen to mock her father. But when she'd woken up from her last barely-a-nap, she'd recognized the brilliance of the queen's disguise.

The queen of Frost had hidden herself entirely by

dressing as a woman of cloth, and no one, not even Ember, had thought to question her. Even when Ember had noticed the change in the person serving her — a change that now she recognized as being from the woman her father, or maybe Shahif, had set to serving her meals to the queen herself — she hadn't thought much of it. It was a new person under those clothes, that head wrap and veil and even gloves, but she hadn't once thought to ask about *who* the new person was.

Her own stupid oversight, she knew now, but it did make for a very effective disguise.

Ember was loath to grant the queen that kind of credit, but she had to admit — it was clever.

And why waste a clever idea? It had worked for the queen to get into the qasun; why shouldn't it work for Ember just as well? The only people besides the Brothers who moved in and out of the 'akhelum were the women of cloth who served them.

To say that the 'akhelum and the qasun were the buildings that made up Sand wasn't strictly true. Just behind the qasun walls a collection of small huts, built of hardened mud bricks that surely melted under even a drizzle of rain. She hadn't given this place much thought since first seeing it, but it was to this bit of Sand where she aimed now.

Because this was the place that housed the women of cloth.

It was midday, and every sensible person was inside to escape from the heat of the sun, and the women of cloth especially were doing their duties in either the qasun or the 'akhelum, so Ember walked through their mud houses without encountering anyone.

She refused to be spooked by the silent not-streets that crisscrossed between the houses, or the crooked, oozing look of the walls around her. It was like nothing she'd ever seen before. Frost was a gleaming city of glass and ice, with buildings that pierced the sky. Dusk was built low to the ground, hunkered into the snow as if hoping the sky wouldn't notice it. The qasun and 'akhelum were there to last, thick walls there to keep sand and sun and storms out.

These buildings were none of those. Ember could pick out several that must've been built during some kind of rain — the walls dripped and then hardened like candle wax. Others leaned dangerously toward their neighbors, one or two even touching and melting into each other. None of the walls were straight. A few were fully collapsed, a hill of hardened mud waiting for the next bit of moisture to turn it back into the ground. The silence of the space, broken only by the rustle of wind through the sand and the mud, made Ember's hair stand on end.

It's only that no one's here, she told herself firmly, setting her jaw against the urge to scream. *They're all at the qasun or the 'akhelum, doing what they do. It wouldn't be so still and silent otherwise.*

It didn't matter that that was true. The quiet spooked her anyway.

She hurried, searching in the spaces between the buildings where she guessed clothes might be set out to dry in the sun. The queen had gotten her hands on a woman of cloth's costume — it couldn't be that difficult to do so.

Between two of the straighter walls in the space, she found them. A full set, it appeared, from veil and gloves to pants and slippers, draped over a rack and set in the sun.

Ember grabbed the whole ensemble and tried to mark the place it had come from. If the buildings around it didn't change too much, she thought she should be able to find it again to return the clothes, maybe with some other, more useful, token of thanks.

All the money she had was Frost coins, but maybe that

could do a woman of cloth some good. Offer her a pull from the beer straw, at least.

She hurried out of the womens' town as fast as she could, eager to escape the silence and disturbing shapes of the walls.

Once clear of everywhere that might be able to look out at her, Ember dressed. She was used to covering herself from head to foot — it was the only way to survive the streets of Dusk, after all — but the black fabric in the scorching heat of the desert was altogether a different thing. Sweat immediately beaded on her forehead, and the cloth held it away from the drying wind until it dripped and skidded into her eyes. The veil obscured her vision more than she'd even expected it to, so she had to squint and focus in order to see anything through the cloth. The gloves made her fingers clumsy and unsure, and the slippers offered very little protection from the burning heat of the sand.

But after a few minutes of dressing and adjusting, Ember was covered from the top of her head to the bottoms of her feet, not even her eyes visible from the outside. She left her usual clothes there, pinned to the ground with a couple of rocks, slipped her compass into the waistband of the new pants, and turned toward the 'akhelum again.

Chapter Sixteen

EMBER WASN'T sure what to expect when she reached the 'akhelum door. She reminded herself with every footfall that, no matter what, she couldn't make a sound. The women of cloth didn't speak — the queen didn't count, she wasn't really a woman of cloth — so no matter how the Brothers spoke to her, she couldn't answer back, or she'd break her disguise.

She checked her veil, her shirt, touched the compass at her waist, making sure there wasn't a slice of skin visible from outside her clothes, and knocked on the door.

Did women of cloth knock when entering the 'akhelum? Well, it was too late to do anything about it now.

The peephole slid open, and a Brother's dirty, unshaven face peeked out. He scowled at Ember, who, grateful suddenly for the cover of the veil, bit her lip and reminded herself not to make a sound.

"Woman," the Brother hissed. "You're late."

Ember didn't move. The sting of teeth in her lip kept her from answering.

The Brother opened the door and waved her inside. "Well. Get in here if you must, but I should report your lateness."

Ember started to move past him into the building, but froze when his hand darted out and grabbed at her tunic. He poked a finger at the back of her neck — his fingernail scraped unevenly against her skin, raising gooseflesh on her arms.

The Brother swiped his finger back and forth across the back of Ember's neck, searching blindly for something he apparently wasn't finding. "Where's your brand?"

Brand?

Ember bit down a little harder on her lip.

The Brother yanked up the bottom edge of her head wrap. Ember pulled away, her hands going to her head to hold the cloth in place, and spun around to face the Brother.

He was leering now, brownish teeth crooked behind his ragged beard. He took a step forward, and his voice dropped to a whisper. "Yes, I know, can't show your face. But how else am I supposed to know which one you are? Show your brand, woman, or I'll find it for you."

Ember tried to think. What could she show this Brother that he'd accept as a brand before he ripped off her veil and revealed her ruse before it had even begun?

She had a scar on her leg. It was an old thing from a childhood accident with an ice pick, barely visible anymore, but the closest thing she had. She rucked up her pant leg, hoping the Dusk dark of her skin wouldn't be too obvious a difference from the Sand dark of his and identify her, and held out the faint puckered line across her calf for the Brother to look at.

He stared down at her leg for a long, silent moment, and Ember couldn't see his face well enough through the veil to tell what he was thinking. Slowly, finally, he looked back up at her. "That's no brand I've ever seen. Who are you?"

Ember lowered her pant leg and wondered how far she could get if she took off down the hall right now. Could she make it to the next corner before this man sprang on her? What sort of alarm could he raise? And how would they react when — it would be *when*, not *if* — they caught her?

She remembered Ahli's expression when he and his fellows had taken her back to the qasun — was it just yesterday? Ember wouldn't put it past him to follow through on his threats of his ax missing the taste of blood.

No, she doubted she'd get far if she ran now. Better to follow through on the plan as she'd made it and play the woman of cloth's role as best she could.

It had gotten her inside the 'akhelum, after all. It was her best chance of getting past this Brother.

And a woman of cloth wouldn't — couldn't? — answer. Ember kept quiet, kept facing him in perfect silence until he remembered that.

"Some foreign tribe, then? Some new outworlder? Pff." The Brother grimaced. "That's what happens when they put spineless *famen* in charge. Rotting outworlders…"

His words weren't for Ember anymore, and they trailed off into incoherent mumbling. She stepped away and started to turn from the Brother, but he caught the motion and grabbed her tunic again.

"Ho now, where're you going?"

Cold raced through Ember's veins, pricking like shards of ice at the undersides of her arms and the crown of her head. An involuntary squeak slid through her teeth before she could catch it.

"I'll be reporting you, like I said. And if I don't recognize your brand, then who should I be reporting, hmm?"

His voice was close. Ember could feel the damp of his breath catching in the cloth over her cheek. She fought back a shudder.

He didn't let go of her collar, instead pushing her down the hall away from the door, further into the 'akhelum.

She was actually a bit taken aback by how plain everything inside the 'akhelum walls looked. Knowing it only by the couple of glimpses she'd had into the dark hallway beyond the door and the blank walls of the outside, perhaps she should've guessed, but its housing of the Spindle always kind of made her think that it was meant to be something a little more interesting inside.

Of course, she didn't even know if the Spindle was meant to be interesting — that was all just speculation on her part, and probably not accurate speculation anyway.

Still, she had expected to see something in the 'akhelum besides the same plain, sand-colored walls and dark, narrow hallways as made up the qasun. At least Papa had filled his own room with carpets and art and places to sit comfortably; the 'akhelum, when the Brother pushing her along in front of them finally picked a room to pull her into, didn't seem to have any of those little luxuries.

This room was as plain and dark as the halls, empty of anything save a large circle scratched into the ground. The Brother skirted her around the circle as they entered, and Ember looked at it while they waited for whatever it was they were waiting for.

It didn't look like much, was nothing but a circle carved deep into the hard bricks of the floor, but the way the Brother avoided it made it obvious that it was important somehow.

She wished she could pull out her compass, find out if

the Spindle was here, if the circle had something to do with it, but she didn't dare. Women of cloth didn't walk around with Before-manufactured compasses looking for the Spindle, so she couldn't, either.

Another person entered the room. Through the dark and the obscured view through her veil, it took Ember a moment to recognize him as Ahli, the leader — she thought — of the Brothers.

"What do you have here, 'akh?" he asked, his voice softer than she'd expected it to be.

"This woman of cloth was late to come, and she won't show her brand."

Don't speak, Ember chanted to herself as the urge to protest rose in her throat. She kept her hands closed into the loosest fists she could manage, rubbing the cloth of her gloves between her fingers.

Ahli turned to her, his tone already hardening. "Well?"

She pulled up the leg of her pants again. Maybe her confidence in the motion would convince Ahli that her childhood scar was just an unfamiliar brand — she didn't let herself think about what it meant that women of cloth were all apparently branded in some way.

He looked at her leg, examined the scar, and Ember held her breath lest she dart for the door or try to insist that she was showing her brand.

Eventually, after a moment that felt longer than some of Ember's weeks, Ahli stepped back. Ember cursed the veil that she still couldn't see his face well enough to guess at what he was thinking.

But she didn't have to wait long for him to say it. He bobbed his head at the other Brother. "I don't know this woman. Fetch the mustafi."

The other Brother scurried off. Ember's heart leaped into her throat.

Ahli stared at her face, and in between cursing the veil for obscuring her vision, she had to toss in a moment of gratitude that it obscured his just as much. She'd done her level best to see through the queen's veil and knew it was impossible, so she risked a smirk at Ahli when he huffed in frustration and shifted back onto his heels.

"Rotting outworlders," he mumbled, though he did pitch his voice loud enough for her to hear, as if deliberately. "If it were up to me, you'd all be the qasun's problem."

Ember smirked again, broader this time.

The first Brother came back trailing a couple of people with him. Brothers mostly, with their scraggly facial hair and naked bodies. One of the people stood out from them, dressed in a fancy tunic and clean-shaven enough that Ember didn't need to squint to see his face.

Eli.

She couldn't run to him, couldn't say or do anything that indicated she even knew him, and it took every ounce of will to remain still and silent.

The room was dim, and she couldn't see well, but she thought she could make out bruises around his eyes and cheeks from where she'd hit him. Again, with every ounce of self-control she had, she kept herself from wincing at the sight. From throwing herself at his feet and begging him to forgive her, if he ever could.

She wouldn't be able to blame him if he couldn't. She'd been not just angry, but cruel. She hadn't even given him a chance to explain himself, to suggest alternatives to how the Brothers had known about their plan. Hadn't given him a moment to even attempt to apologize.

She'd assumed he'd told them, and she'd been as awful as she knew how to be in exacting revenge for it.

And all the while, Felix had been a doll. Ember had

never seen any dolls around the 'akhelum, but if they could communicate with each other, maybe with Papa, even with the queen, was it so strange to think they might be doing the same with the Brothers?

She looked at Eli, at the evidence of her cruelty on his face, and realized that she didn't deserve his forgiveness.

That fact cut deep. Before Frost, she'd never imagined a scenario where she and Eli might not be able to be friends anymore — now, she had several.

And one of them was written in purplish swollen flesh around his eyes.

"Mustafi," Ahli said, interrupting Ember's thoughts. "We're sorry to interrupt you, but we required your wisdom about this woman. None of us recognize her brand."

He stepped back, waved Eli to take his place directly in front of Ember. He, like maybe everyone who came so close to a woman of cloth, peered at her through the veil, obviously trying to make out some feature beneath the cloth.

She wasn't sure if she wanted him to be successful or not. If recognizing her would make him angry or sympathetic. She hated it, this feeling that she didn't know Eli, that she couldn't predict what he would do.

That's what you get for being cruel, she thought, the voice in her head so distinct that it did actually form the words. *He shouldn't forgive you.*

"Show me your brand."

Well, she'd played the ruse this far, and she didn't have any other ideas — no point in not trying her best to keep it up.

She offered him her leg, and he frowned down at it for a moment. Would he recognize it? He'd been with her during that accident, trying to teach her how to climb ice when her pick slipped and cut her, but it was so long ago, and it wasn't the first, or last, time Ember had cut herself in his presence, only the one that made any visible lasting mark.

She had only a second or two to dwell on the question when Eli gasped, his eyes darting back to face.

So. He did recognize it.

The urge to drop to her knees, to take his hands and beg like the terrible creature she was for his forgiveness, nearly overwhelmed her. She'd shifted her weight forward so that her knees would smack sharp and painful against the floor before she remember that she couldn't. Not yet. Not until after Eli told the Brothers exactly who she was and her disguise wouldn't matter anymore.

Then, she promised herself, then once there was truly no hope for getting to the Spindle — she'd do it then. Fall to her knees, to her belly if he wanted, lick his feet — lick the Brothers' feet, even. Anything. Anything he wanted to prove that she was sorry, truly, deeply sorry.

Silence stretched like an overwrought belt, creaky gears and rusty nails struggling for purchase. Tears were already building behind her eyes, waiting for the moment they were free to fall, but Ember kept them contained for now. For a terribly long moment, she and Eli looked at each other, though of course he couldn't see her beneath the veil. But he knew who he was seeing; recognition was obvious in his bruised face. Her apology bubbled with the tears in her throat.

She could only hope it would be enough.

Eli broke the silence at last. "Ah." It was more a throat-clear than a word. He turned to Ahli and the other waiting Brothers. "Yes. I know this brand. It's the Farways."

"Farways?" Ahli repeated, suspicion heavy in his tone.

"They come from up north. From outside of Dusk,

actually. That's why you've never seen them before, because I wouldn't ever think someone that far to the north would make it down here. Well." A grin entered his tone. "It's possible, obviously. But I can't imagine it's very common. Most people don't survive the tundra long enough to get anywhere, you know."

Ahli grunted, and Ember wasn't sure if it was meant to be acknowledgment or not. "So, you know this woman?"

"I know her brand. That … was the problem, wasn't it?"

"Mmm."

"I'll just see her to her place. Um. You're all dismissed."

Ahli grunted again, but it seemed he wasn't keen on arguing with Eli. The Brothers left, though Ahli lingered behind.

"Any progress?" he asked, in a voice low enough that Ember knew he wasn't looking to be overheard.

"Have some patience," Eli answered, and while the words came out steady, it was clear to Ember that he was bluffing, just as he had been since recognizing her.

"I have. And I'm beginning to suspect you're a fraud start to end."

Don't speak, don't speak. The chant was almost background noise in her head by now, fading away from the front of her consciousness to make it almost difficult to remember. Fortunately, it came roaring back as she opened her mouth to jump in and defend Eli from whatever accusation the Brother was making.

"I'll find it. Today, I think."

"Today, then."

Ahli swept out of the room.

When Eli turned back around, his eyes were wide and his shoulders hunching in — he was shaken by that exchange with Ahli. Then he shook his head, pulled in a breath, and straightened back to his natural height. "Ember," he whispered.

"Hi," she whispered back and reached to take off the veil, but Eli put a hand on her arm and stopped her.

"No. It's a good idea. Don't ruin it yet."

She dropped her hand but couldn't hold back the words anymore. "Eli." His name came out as a sob. "Eli, I'm so sorry. I never … I can't…"

There were too many words, too much to apologize for — she didn't know where to start.

"I'm so sorry," she repeated. "I'm so, so sorry."

Eli patted her shoulder, but he didn't say anything, either to tell her she wasn't forgiven, or to say that she was. Instead, he changed the subject.

"You're here about the Spindle."

Ember sucked in a breath and tried to collect herself, grateful once again for the veil that hid how difficult that actually was. If he didn't want to talk about it right now, that would be up to him. She'd do whatever he needed — apologize, grovel, or change the subject entirely. "Obviously."

"Have you found it?"

"It's inside these walls, I'm sure of it. Somewhere on the southwestern side." She pulled out her compass. It was swinging a little, but only a little and holding that south-west direction as the anchor for its swing.

Eli took the compass from her gloved fingers. "Isn't this…?"

She nodded. "It's been pointing to the Spindle the entire time, only sometimes the Spindle isn't even there. I don't know why. I wish I did."

Eli tilted the compass this way and that, his eyes on the needle and his bottom lip caught between his teeth in thought. When he lowered it enough for Ember to see the face of it again, the needle was spinning in lazy circles around the entire dial.

"What did you—" she started to ask, but then cut herself off as she caught the tone of her voice. She, of all the people in the world, had the least right to yell at Eli for anything. But she did take back the compass, careful not to snatch at it.

The needle steadied in her hand, still not falling back into a single spot, but no longer making complete circles.

"It's meant for you," Eli said. "The Brothers have been calling me their savior, but I'm not. I think you might be."

Chapter Seventeen

EMBER FOLLOWED Eli through the 'akhelum. Though they were really following the compass, Eli said it would look strange for him to let a woman of cloth lead and to keep up the disguise, he would have to be a step ahead and holding the compass most of the time. Just in case a Brother came by, they didn't want to give away Ember's ruse. The Brothers were all expecting Eli to take this wayward woman to her proper place and see that she was properly punished for being late, after all. They wouldn't, he promised, question Ember again.

Eli holding the compass did make following it a bit of a challenge. He knew how to handle of compass, but this one acted up every time he touched it. Still, Ember knew they were headed for the southwest side of the 'akhelum, and as they got closer to the wall where she'd found the Spindle before, they paused every few steps so Ember could hold the compass, wait for it to steady, and point them in the right direction.

For several minutes, they paced back and forth in this manner through one empty hall, until handing the compass back to Eli got annoying enough that Ember couldn't keep it down. "Is anyone coming?"

"No. This hallway's usually empty."

She held out her hand. "Well, then, let me have it."

He gave her the compass but wasn't finished. "I'm telling you, this isn't the right spot. We passed it two turns ago."

Ember wasn't listening. She pulled off the veil and watched the compass.

"Ember, you can't—"

"I can't see through all that cloth. Just tell me if anyone's coming."

She moved slowly, watching for the minute changes in the compass's position that indicated she was in the right place. With her free hand, she caressed the wall.

"The room where they keep it is back there. I know — I've been waiting for something to appear in it for days."

"Shh."

She was close, she could feel it. The pull inside her had never been stronger, never been closer to where it wanted her to go. But she couldn't feel anything properly with her clothed hands. She paused a moment, tore one glove off with her teeth, and then pressed it bare back against the wall.

"This is a wall, Ember. Nothing more. There aren't even rooms here."

"Shh!"

The compass needle was still swinging, slowly, and inside only a few degrees of space, but not locking onto a spot regardless. She looked up at Eli, hovering near her shoulder.

"Step back."

"What—"

"Step back. It won't come with you here."

It seemed almost obvious once she had the thought. The Spindle came when she was there, but when only she was. When she tried to show it to Papa, when the Brothers were around, it wasn't there. The times when she'd been unable to find it when she was by herself at the southwestern wall, someone must've been nearby, in the hallway, or somehow otherwise too close.

But as soon as she said it, the last little piece of the whole thing clicked into place. The Spindle, the Leshii, had been pulling at, calling out, to her.

Her — not Papa, or Eli, or the Brothers. She was the one meant to find it.

Eli stepped back from her shoulder, one step, then two. The compass needle stabilized, and Ember once again touched her fingers to the wall.

"I'm here," she whispered, too quiet to echo against the stone. "It's your turn."

A crack appeared in the wall beneath her fingers. It grew and widened and opened up into the Spindle.

FOR A MOMENT, Ember could do nothing but stare, her jaw loose from surprise and awe. She'd seen things before that amazed her — Frost's electric lights and grand machines came to mind — but this was something entirely different. More than just science she didn't understand, but like her entire life had suddenly found focus and meaning like it never had before.

She wasn't sure at first exactly what she was looking at. The Spindle, of course, but what it *was* didn't exactly make sense on first glance. It looked like a room viewed through an archway of 'akhelum stone that had formed beneath her fingertips, but a room like nothing she'd ever seen before, trimmed in gleaming gold and bright with sunlight even though there were no windows inside it. In the center was a tightly spiraled staircase that quickly disappeared into the floor.

Ember moved toward the room, toward the stairs, understanding without needing to be told that was what she was supposed to do. Dimly, she heard Eli's voice speaking to her, saying something that didn't register in her head.

It didn't matter. Nothing had ever mattered except this place.

Slowly, aware that she was stepping onto hallowed ground, Ember moved past the 'akhelum wall and into the room.

She didn't want to waste time, but she also didn't want to rush. She traced her fingers across a couple of the shimmering gold trimmings of the room, letting herself feel the delicate swirls and intricate designs of the space before moving to the steps. Something inside her, beneath her, around her, hummed, and her whole self felt alive. Alight and brimming with something greater than happiness, bigger than joy.

She couldn't name it. She didn't know how to try. She just allowed herself to sink into it, to sweep her down the stairs toward her purpose in life.

Every couple of steps opened up into another room. Each of them was as different from the sunlight gold of the first as that room was from her home in Dusk. In one room, she saw a statue of a man holding up the entire world on his back, and she barely had time to wonder at the other parts of that world before the next room had windows that looked out onto mountains full of crystalline lakes and running streams. Another was made up of plants — real living plants as green as she could imagine and spotted all through with flowers of every color. Another was full of mechanics, gears and wires and electrics that would make her scientist parts weep, and one more wasn't a room at all, but an open plain of sandy yellow grass and nothing else.

Ember took in as much as she could, but she knew even as she walked that she was missing most of it. That more rooms, more things, were opening up to her than she could possibly see and understand in a lifetime, never mind the mere moments she gave it as she spiraled down the stairs.

But, as fascinating as any one of those places would surely be, she knew she was headed for the bottom.

Someday, she promised herself as she passed by a view of the inner workings of some machine. Someday, when she had the time, she would come back here. She would enter each and every one of these rooms. She would learn their secrets, understand their meanings.

She would find out what the Spindle actually *was.*

For now, though, she could only peek in and marvel.

She came to the bottom of the steps at last. Unlike all the other places on this staircase, the bottom room was empty and dark. Ember paused, catching her breath, trying to blink away the thoughts of the other rooms that clung like an afterimage of light to the insides of her eyelids.

"H-hello?" she whispered into the darkness. Her voice echoed dully as if there was nothing around at all to hold onto the sound.

She wasn't expecting an answer, but she got one anyway.

Help me.

Her compass, held mostly forgotten in one hand, was vibrating from the force of the needle's motion.

She started toward the sound. It was difficult — the noise, barely even a voice, came at her from every direction at once — but she picked what felt like the right direction and aimed toward it anyway.

That pull inside her hadn't steered her wrong yet; there was no reason to assume it would now.

Ember had taken only a few steps into the darkness when she glimpsed it.

At first, she thought it was some kind of building, taller and narrower than anything she'd seen in Frost, but what else could it be? But as her eyes adjusted and her vision cleared, she saw the giant structure before her was not a building, but a machine.

No, not a machine. An engine. *The* Engine.

It rose so high into the air Ember couldn't see the top of it, and what of its innards she could see through rusty holes in its plating showed gears that matched together almost too perfectly to be real. But the whole thing was silent and broken, plates rusting and belts dusty and cracked.

Help me.

The words were coming from inside the Engine itself, not as words, but as a feeling, a plea to live again, to work as it was meant to work.

Ember stepped up to it. She wanted to reach out, touch it, tell it that she was here, she had found it at last, but that would be like touching a god — something no mortal should be allowed to do.

But she did have the courage to name it. "Leshii," she whispered.

The ground rumbled beneath her feet.

"I'm here," she said, as if that could possibly matter to a god. "What should I do? How can I help?"

She was no one — a Dusk girl who liked to tinker with mechanics. The daughter of the scientist who might actually be able to do what the engine needed. But she wanted to help. She hated seeing this engine still and silent, and if there was something she could do, some way she could help, that would be more than she'd ever dared to hope for in her life.

Touch me. Listen.

The urge to run her fingers along those metal plates, to knock the rust off the gears, was suddenly too much to keep down. And if the engine wanted that, who was she, a mere girl, to argue?

She brushed her fingertips, then her palms, along one flat face of the engine's plating. And she listened.

At first, there was nothing. No sound, not even imagined sound, for her to listen to. But then the images came, fast as a dream, a nightmare. She'd seen them all before, the terrible end of the Leshii, the destruction that changed Before into now, but she'd never seen them with such clarity and feeling. She'd never shared the Leshii's death scream with it, the pain of struggling to hold on while the world tore you apart.

The Leshii howled, and she howled with it.

"What's that? Who's there?"

It was a voice — another voice, human, interrupting the dark. Ember spun around. She had time to register the shape of another person behind her before everything went black.

Chapter Eighteen

EMBER STAGGERED as the hand pressing on her shoulder shoved her to her knees. The floor beneath them was hard, and the drop sent little shivers of pain racing up her legs. The bag over her head, coarse-woven and smelling like it usually lived in the Brothers' armpits, didn't let her see anything but the sliver of light that crept underneath it. Her bound hands kept her from being able to rip it off.

She didn't know where she was other than still inside the 'akhelum. By the noises around her, it seemed to be a large, echoey room full of other people, and those other people — Brothers, undoubtedly — were angry. Shouts rang from the walls, bounced against the ceiling, shivered through the floor and into Ember's bones.

As awful as the bag over her head was for obscuring her vision and filling her nose with the unpleasant scent of the Brothers, she was glad of it the same way she'd been of the woman of cloth's veil — it kept anyone from seeing her fear.

At least until the Brother moving her around tore it off

her head, catching and yanking at a couple of loose hairs in the process.

It was a little thing, the sting of a few hairs being torn out at the root, but it felt like a warning of worse to come.

Ember blinked in the sudden brightness of the room ablaze with candles and electric lights, and it took her eyes a moment to adjust from the darkness of the Leshii and the smelly bag and make out the shapes in front of her.

"Look who I found lurking around our engine," the Brother at her shoulder said, to another round of angry shouts from the others lining the walls.

Ahli stepped forward out of the crowd. "Qasunfi. What did I tell you about seeing your face again?"

Ember didn't answer — that wasn't the sort of question she was supposed to answer, and it didn't feel like a good idea to open her mouth at all.

Ahli turned around and held out a hand to another Brother, and when he turned back, he held a large blade in his hand. Ember didn't recognize the shape of it — it wasn't one of her own familiar single-edged knives, or even a double-sided dagger like was a relatively common artifact from Before. Instead, this blade was squat and wedge-shaped, its face tapering to a wide single edge at the opposite side of the short, fat handle.

Ember didn't recognize the shape, but it didn't take much to work out what it was for. A heavy, wedge-shaped blade like that was made to separate things: cracking rocks, splintering wood, and generally cutting parts off a whole sturdy sort of structure.

Ahli swung the blade up to rest on his shoulder as he approached her. His expression was thoughtful, but his eyes were cold with fury.

Ember struggled against the rope holding her hands behind her, but the wrap was tight, the knots unyielding.

The rope was coarse — she could already feel the places where the skin was rubbing raw beneath it.

Ahli knelt in front of her, stared into her eyes. There was no feeling there but that icy rage, a brutal sort of madness devoid of care or mercy.

"We've been very patient with you," he said at last, his voice almost inaudible through the echoing voices of the others in the room. "Most qasunfi would've felt the fullness of our wrath the first time we caught them lurking around us, but for you, we've let that wrath slide, kept it to ourselves lest I lead the Brothers into an all-out war with that impostor prince. But we warned you, qasunfi. Again and again, we warned you to stay away. Our patience has finally worn thin."

Ember couldn't keep her eyes off the chopping blade at his shoulder. Her voice came out cracked and small, unrecognizable. "Please. I mean you no harm."

This pulled a laugh, first from Ahli, then from the others in the room. The Brother at her shoulder cackled practically into her ear.

Ahli stood. He met the eyes of the Brother at Ember's shoulder and nodded once, and the Brother yanked at her arms out straight behind her. She fell forward in an effort to keep her elbows from snapping, landing on the floor with an unpleasant thwack, and the Brother rolled her onto her side and held her arms pinned to the ground behind her.

Ahli shifted out of view. "Hold her still."

If Ember had ever been afraid before, it was nothing to what she felt now. Panic raced down her limbs, and she tried to struggle away from the Brother's grip, to wiggle her wrists free of their bonds, to find any kind of purchase in her thin cloth slippers on the floor. But the Brother leaned his weight against her shoulder and arms, pinning her to her side on the floor, and a moment later, someone else was doing the same to her ankles so she couldn't move even enough to see what was happening.

"Please. Please don't!"

She'd never thought she'd be the sort of person who would beg and sob in fear, but here she was, sobbing breathlessly and begging into the hard, dirty floor of the room under the ceaseless jeers of a terrible audience.

Ahli didn't answer. Neither did the other Brothers holding her down. For a long moment, they were all still and silent, and Ember couldn't see them, couldn't see anything through the haze of terror but that hard, dirty floor.

Then Ahli's blade whistled faintly through the air and landed hard against her bound wrists.

PAIN.

Ember had known what it was most of her life. All people of Dusk knew pain, the different forms it took, the subtle varieties of it. She knew the gnawing emptiness of a hungry belly and the dull throb of hopelessness. She knew the sharp agony of a broken bone and the endless all-over ache of illness. The icy shards of panic, the restlessness of paranoia, the constant prickle of maybe freezing tonight — it was all part and parcel of her life.

At its core, Dusk was made up of people too stubborn to die when the world ended, and that had created a vast variety of different sorts of pain, from injuries and illnesses to bad nights where it seemed like morning might never come, or if it did, it wouldn't make any sort of difference.

Ember thought she knew pain in just about every form it could take, but nothing had prepared her for this.

For several long moments, there was no pain at all.

She heard the noise of Ahli's blade cutting through the air, felt the sharp edge hit her wrists — particularly her right, which was the one on top — but wasn't entirely sure what had happened. She couldn't see anything but the floor and a couple of Brothers' bare feet and dirty toes. Even their shouts seemed far away, as if coming at her from across the desert. But there was no pain, even though Ahli had undoubtedly struck her with the sharp end of his blade.

And then the Brother at her shoulders shifted her right arm. She felt the limb slip free of the rope binding her wrists, and the pain came.

Ember gasped. She'd never felt anything like it before. Even the time she'd broken her ankle and spent an entire winter limping around on a homemade crutch was nothing like this. That had been a sharp agony, then months of unrelenting ache, but it had also been mostly contained to her broken ankle. This pain spread from her wrist up her arm, then into her spine and head. Little black dots threatened the corners of her vision.

And it wasn't just her right arm — her left hurt, too, a little less badly, but it was with her left hand that she could feel the blood. It pulsed across her palm, fast and hot. Her left hand burned like she'd stuck it into a fire.

Why couldn't she feel her right hand? Why was the blood pouring into her left palm but not her right? Why were her left fingers burning, but the pain ended at the wrist of her right hand? The way it was shooting from her wrist to her spine and back seemed like it shouldn't spare her hand.

She couldn't see. She tried to turn, but the Brothers' grips on her arms and ankles wouldn't let her, and she couldn't crane her neck around enough to see what was happening. When she tried, all she could catch was the sight of Ahli's blade, already bloody, raised above his shoulder again, preparing for a second strike.

The noise of a door being wrenched open, footsteps rushing across the floor, interrupted the shouts and jeers from the crowd. Ahli dropped his blade, but not onto Ember's hands again, but to the floor, and the noises from the crowd died.

"What's all this, then?" came a voice from underneath the sounds of footsteps. "All of you collected together just for my convenience? That's very thoughtful, but quite unnecessary."

Papa.

Papa was here.

He'd come to rescue her.

Ember thrashed against her captors, and this time their grips on her limbs loosened enough that she could slide out from under them. The black spots in her vision threatened to claim her, but she squeezed her eyes shut so she wouldn't have to see them, gritted her teeth, and breathed through the pain. The blood was flowing unimpeded, and for a moment, she wasn't sure she'd be able to hold onto consciousness long enough to sit up and find out what Ahli had done to her.

But Papa was here for her. She had to get up.

Slowly, fighting against the pain that threatened to sink her, Ember moved. Pulled her legs away from the hold of the Brother at her ankles. Shifted her arms out of the hold of that Brother as well. Sobs banged at the back of her teeth, a few especially slippery ones escaping their cage and making it out into the world, but she couldn't hold down everything at once, there wasn't enough room inside her to contain all of it.

The floor was slippery with blood. Her feet skidded as she tried to get them under her, tried to prop herself up.

She could still feel it pouring into her left hand, pulsing onto the ground, leaking in a widening circle from her no-longer-bound wrists. It matted in her hair, smeared across her face, filled her nose and mouth with its distinct metal-and-salt tang.

At last, she was able to get her feet to respond to her, to pull her legs up enough that she could prop herself onto her knees. She looked up, still avoiding the sight of her hands, still not ready to see what Ahli had done to her.

Papa was coming down the middle of the room. He carried several different devices — one of which Ember recognized as the box he'd used to command the doll to take away the queen, but the others, though similarly sized and shaped, were unfamiliar to her. He worked them quickly, switching from one to the other in rapid succession, never dropping one because she realized that they were attached to his arms and waist.

Behind him, around him, protecting him, responding subtly to his use of his control devices, were dolls. More dolls than there were Brothers in the room, more dolls than Ember had ever seen in a single place before. And by the sounds of footsteps in the hallway, there were many more dolls coming.

Ember scanned their faces, not sure if she was looking for or looking to avoid the one doll she wasn't ready to find. She recognized a couple of them — one doll from her weeks working on them in Frost, memorable for the way her madness had manifested in a willingness to actually talk; another who had served her breakfast in a café; perhaps even the trolley driver who'd crashed into Frost's southern wall, turned the crack into a proper hole.

A flash of red snagged at the corner of her vision. Ember turned away from it. Told herself it meant nothing.

Ahli took the final step that brought him almost toe-to-

toe with Papa. He didn't raise his blade, but the muscles in his arms tensed as though he was thinking about it. "Mikail." He spat over Papa's name.

Papa didn't even look up from his devices. "Hello, Ahli."

"You're not welcomed here."

"Hence the need to break in." Papa didn't sound concerned, or even all that interested, with anything Ahli was about to say or do.

Ahli hefted his chopping blade, first to his shoulder, then up above his head, and furious intent shone from every muscle and bone inside the Brother's body.

"NO!" Ember screamed.

The blade fell as if in slow motion toward Papa's head. But before it could strike anything, a doll was there, knocking the blade aside with one hand and, in almost the same motion, grabbing Ahli's head and twisting it sharply to one side.

Ahli's eyes went wide for a single second, his mouth opening in a soundless cry, and then he crumpled to the floor, as lifeless as a powered-off doll. His blade cracked against the floor at the same time.

Papa never even looked up. He spoke low and emotionless to the room. "Don't challenge me again, or you'll be joining your 'akh in the afterlife.

"Now." He straightened, and, for the first time, looked up from his devices, around at the roomful of Brothers. "I believe the Spindle has been found?"

Chapter Nineteen

NONE of the Brothers answered Papa's question. They looked at the dolls, those around Papa and those still coming into the room, looked at their crumpled-up leader, and knew better than to speak at all.

It took everything, every ounce of will and strength she had left, but Ember was able at last to get to her feet. The black spots flashed across her vision — she squeezed her eyes shut again and breathed until they retreated.

"Papa." Her voice was a whisper, ragged and desperate.

He looked at her for the first time, scanned her from head to toe. She knew she was a mess, dirty and hurt, unable to look at her hands even as she felt the blood still leaking freely from the place Ahli had landed his blade, barely holding on to conscious thought by sheer Dusk stubbornness. Her mouth was sticky, tacky with the blood drying inside it. Even her spit tasted like blood and sick.

His gaze stuck on her hands, and his entire expression wrinkled in disgust and horror.

"Papa?" she said again, this time as a question, a whimper, a plea.

He'd come for her. He had. That's why he was here, to rescue her from the second swing of that blade. He hadn't made it in time to prevent the first, but he'd stopped the second. He'd come for her.

He loved her.

He did.

His presence here, his rescue, proved it.

He turned away.

She couldn't avoid it any longer — the need to know finally overwhelmed the fear of finding out. She sagged back against the wall, pulled in a few steadying breaths, and looked at her hands.

The left one was cut terribly at the inside of her wrist, the slice deep enough to expose muscle and bone. The hand slumped awkwardly, and when she tried to move it, to wiggle her fingers or rotate her wrist, nothing responded.

Her right hand was missing altogether.

It took Ember a moment to fully process that fact, to go from seeing it to understanding it. To register that was why she hadn't felt the blood on her right palm, why her right hand slid so easily from the rope that had a moment before held both her wrists so firmly together.

Ahli's chopping blade had removed her right hand from her body. He would've taken her left hand completely, too, had he been allowed to make that second swing.

Strangely, as the fact of what she was seeing settled into her mind, it didn't come with pain, with horror, with anything at all. Numbness spread through her, and it was almost soothing, the caress of nothing after too much of everything.

There was someone at her shoulder. A doll, one she

didn't know. It put a hand on her arm, and Ember couldn't feel it. She couldn't feel anything.

"Come," the doll said, not harshly, but not gently, either.

It, too, felt nothing.

It waited, but Ember couldn't move. Couldn't feel her feet, couldn't remember what it meant to walk. The doll waited, but then it stopped waiting. It bent over and swept Ember's legs out from under her, lifting her up in its arms.

The jolt almost brought sensation back to her, almost offended her. Didn't it know how hard it had been to get her feet under her control? Why was it taking that away again?

But that was too hard. It was too hard to feel, and she was so tired.

Ember leaned her head against the doll's shoulder and didn't protest as the doll turned around and jogged out of the room, away from Papa, away from the Brothers. It smelled like nothing. She felt nothing, not even pain, as the doll carried her away.

SHE DIDN'T FADE into unconsciousness — her body wouldn't be that kind to her to allow that — but Ember did lose track of where and why she was enough that when a hand touched her shoulder, it startled her out of a daze.

In the minutes or months of numbness, the fresh agony of her injuries had faded, but the ache that replaced it was not an improvement. She blinked and struggled to focus on her surroundings — difficult, because everything was tilted sideways and none of it made sense.

A person hovered above her. Ember started to pull away but found she didn't have the strength to do even that.

If the person wanted to hurt her, kill her, they should just do it now while Ember couldn't fight back.

The person crouched down, and her face came into view.

The queen.

Ember closed her eyes. The queen had been out for her from the beginning, and now she was caught. Injured past the ability to fight her off. Useless.

The word rang in her ears.

Useless. Useless. Useless.

Storms had showed her her worst fears, of her hands withering, making her useless to everyone around her.

And now it had come true. All she had was her hands, to fix what was broken and find what was lost.

Now, she wouldn't even be able to hold her compass.

Papa had seen it right away, even before she'd worked up the nerve to see it herself. He'd taken one look at her and turned away, disgusted. Dismissive.

Disappointed.

He's sent his doll to bring Ember into the same room with the queen. His enemy. His captive.

Did that make Ember his enemy, his captive, too?

"Ember?"

The word came from far away — from outside her head, barely loud enough to cut through her thoughts. The queen's voice, cold and blue.

Ember burrowed her face into the cushion or pillow or whatever it was keeping her head off the otherwise-hard floor beneath the rest of her. Even the soft place beneath her head was sticky with blood.

The queen had told her to fix her machines, her dolls. Machines that weren't broken, dolls that were only responding to new orders.

She'd been useless from the start. Should've been left to wither away in the darkness.

"Why?"

It was the only thing left that mattered.

"Why what?" The queen's voice was soft, but that didn't make it warm, or gentle, or kind.

Ember missed kind. She missed Felix.

Unless he would be disgusted by her, too, now, a useless, bloody shell of what she should be.

That way lay more pain. She couldn't handle that now. She answered the queen instead. "Why did you make me leave?"

"I never made you do anything."

"I didn't have to leave Frost."

"No."

"You made me suspicious."

"I never made you do anything."

But Ember would never forget the way her Envoys threatened her friends. How, on a single nod from her, one of them had stuck a knife into Eli's side because Ember's help displeased her.

She'd gone to Frost of her own free will, but that was the last time she'd done anything free of the manipulations of others.

"You kidnapped my friends. Hurt them."

"I thought it was necessary."

"But I told you it wasn't."

"Ember."

She didn't like the tone the queen was taking, but didn't know how to stop it.

"My people trust me to keep them safe from the outside world. I will do whatever it takes to not betray that trust. If it means keeping secrets or … motivating an outworlder the only way they'll be motivated, I'll do that."

Ember almost scoffed at her choice of words — motivating, indeed — but that took effort and a sense of humor that she didn't deserve to have.

She stayed quiet instead.

"Let me see your hands."

Ember pulled her arms to her chest instead. The last thing she needed was for the rotting queen of Frost to get a good look at her injuries.

"We have to stop the bleeding." The blue ice came back into her tone. "Unless you fancy dying slowly and painfully here on a Sand floor."

It was better than Ember deserved, really. At least she was near Papa. Knew that he was alive and well. However he felt about her, she was glad to know that.

But if she were to die here, she would rather it be something a little quicker than bleeding out from Ahli's blade. And she couldn't do anything about the bleeding herself, with one hand gone and the other hanging useless by only half its bones.

She didn't trust the queen, but she wasn't sure what other choice she had. She didn't, in fact, fancy dying like this, slow and weak and crumpled.

Ember relaxed her arms, and when the queen took the right one by the elbow, she didn't pull away.

The queen looked over the stump that used to be Ember's right wrist. The blue paint she used to wear on her lips and eyelids was gone, but there was still a faint blue cast to her skin. Whether it was stained from the paint or if her skin just looked like that naturally, Ember wasn't sure. Her fingers were cold and steady.

"There's no way to bandage that," the queen decided after a moment. "We'll have to go with a tourniquet."

She released Ember's arm, looked around the room but didn't see what she was hoping for, and sighed loudly.

"This is absurd, Mikail," she said, out loud but only to the air in front of her. "You could at least give me something to work with."

She frowned down at the long tunic and pants she was still wearing from her woman of cloth disguise. With a little bit of finagling, she was able to work her fingers into a loose seam and tear a strip of cloth off the hem, then turned back to Ember, still frowning. "Absurd."

The queen wrapped the strip of cloth around Ember's arm, just above her elbow. Ember tried not to flinch, but every nerve in her right arm burned, and even the touch of cloth felt like it was laced with little shards of glass.

The cloth looped around her arm twice, the queen pulling it tight on both turns. She started to knot it, but halfway through the knot stood up, the loose ends of the cloth still clutched in her hands so she was bent almost in half, and set her foot lightly on Ember's elbow.

She looked Ember in the eye, and there was a glimmer of something like sympathy there beneath the usual cold in her gaze. "This won't feel good."

Once again, Ember almost scoffed but couldn't quite manage it. She'd just had one hand completely chopped off — nothing felt good. But she took the warning for what it was and braced herself against a fresh wave of pain.

The queen pulled hard at the ends of the cloth, and Ember understood why she'd stood up, why she'd pinned Ember's arm beneath her foot — so that she could get leverage and force into the motion.

Ember gritted her teeth and didn't let herself cry out, but noises still escaped her throat regardless.

It wasn't as bad as the blade had been. She doubted anything could be. But the pressure squeezed her skin and muscle tight to her upper arm bone, set her burning nerves alight. At first, she could feel blood pulsing through the spot, struggling to make it past the place where the veins were being cut off, but then even blood couldn't make it through the cloth — a tourniquet, the queen had called it. Her forearm tingled for a moment, then went numb.

The queen pressed her toe to the start of the knot to hold it where it was, then finished it quickly before it could loosen and sat back on her heels to examine her work.

Ember dared a look, too. The flow of blood from her stump had slowed to a trickle.

"Hopefully, you won't lose even more of your arm," was the only thing the queen said.

Ember closed her eyes. The sight of her handless wrist brought all those black spots rushing across her vision again.

The queen tore a couple more strips off her tunic and wrapped Ember's left wrist more conventionally, tight enough to hurt but not to block her blood deep inside her wrist.

"Rest now," the queen said after finishing her second arm. "You'll feel better after you've rested."

Ember doubted that, but opening her eyelids suddenly felt about as possible as regrowing her hand, and she welcomed the nothingness of sleep.

Chapter Twenty

IT WASN'T GOOD SLEEP, not restful or peaceful. The pain and fear of the last she'd-lost-track-of-time followed her even into unconsciousness and never let her slip further than a light doze.

But, loathe as she was to admit the queen had been right, Ember did feel better when she woke up again, this time to the click of a lock and creak of a door hinge. At least, her head felt a little clearer, her eyes a little easier to focus, her body a little more under her control.

The queen was standing at the doorway, her body blocking the view of whoever was at the door so all Ember could see was the strip of light from the hall and the queen's shadow.

"Let her rest," the queen whispered.

"I brought tea."

"Shahif!" Ember said before the queen could answer. She tried to sit up, but the wooziness that overwhelmed her warned that she wasn't ready for that much motion yet.

Shahif stepped past the queen, who followed his movement with a scowl but didn't protest, and he knelt in front of Ember. He was indeed carrying a steaming cup, and Ember recognized the smell coming off it as the same kind of tea he'd brought her after the storm.

Ember rolled to her side. The bleeding had mostly stopped while she dozed, but her entire right arm from the tourniquet down was now completely numb and flopped out of her control when she moved her shoulder. Her left hand was throbbing, and she couldn't move any of her fingers.

Shahif stared, then saw Ember notice his staring and turned his gaze away. Not like Papa had, in disgust and dismissal, but like he didn't want to remind her of what had happened.

"It's okay if you need to stare," Ember mumbled.

"I brought you tea."

She smiled. Even that hurt — her lips were dry and cracked. "To heal both body and mind?"

"It worked before."

She couldn't argue with that. She started to reach for the cup but hesitated when she remembered that she wouldn't be able to hold it, that even the fingers she did have weren't responding to her control.

Her stomach sank at this new understanding of how useless she was now.

Shahif seemed to realize the same thing at the same time. He set the cup down and shifted toward her head, one hand opened toward her like he intended to slide it behind her head and prop her up.

Ember swallowed down the humiliation and didn't protest when Shahif did just that, lifting her head and settling it against his elbow so she wasn't completely flat on the floor, then bringing the cup to her lips himself.

Ember drank. The tea was too hot to drink comfortably, but she wanted this whole thing over with as quickly as possible, so she swallowed it in gulps and let it burn her tongue and throat as it went down.

Shahif set her back down once the tea was gone, and even though the whole thing had been terrible, Ember knew he'd helped her. "Thank you."

"You're not the first. Likely won't be the last."

Not the first person who'd lost their hands to the Brothers' chopping blade, or not the first person Shahif had helped after such an injury? She didn't press for clarification, though fresh curiosity prickled through her thoughts.

Shahif had been a Brother — she'd gathered enough about him to guess that. She wondered what else he knew, what else he'd seen and experienced inside the 'akhelum, what he was doing here, now, in the qasun.

"Is there anything else I can do?" Shahif looked up from Ember to include the queen in his question.

The queen had been hovering, unobtrusive but still scowling, just behind Shahif. "Don't speak of this to Mikail," she said like that was an answer to his question.

"Clearly."

"Then you've done enough. You can go now."

Shahif shifted to get to his feet, presumably to obey the queen's order, but Ember didn't want him to leave, to let her alone with the queen who, yes, had helped her before, but that hardly meant she was on Ember's side. She had her own motives, her own desires, and Ember didn't know what they were and if they included not hurting her further.

The queen of Frost would do whatever she had to to get her way, and Ember didn't know what her way was.

"Wait," she said before Shahif had finished standing. He settled back onto his knees, and Ember cast around for something he could help her do. "M-my compass."

She pressed her left arm to the secret pocket at her

waist where she'd put the compass back as she went down the Spindle stairs and huffed a sigh of relief to feel it pressing back.

"If you could just…" She let the request fade off, suddenly aware that she was asking Shahif to lift her tunic and reach into her waistband.

Well, there was nothing for it. She couldn't take the compass out herself.

He did it quickly, without hesitating in any way that might make the gesture seem embarrassing or lewd, plucking the compass out of her pocket and resting it on her palm without even having to be asked for that second part.

It felt good. Normal. The metal casing was cool against the over-warm skin of her hand, and even though the pressure of something touching her hand made her entire arm burn, she could ignore the pain for the sense of normalcy holding the compass offered. She wished she could close her fingers around it, squeeze it until everything else went away and it was just her and this silly trinket, the last sign she would ever have of her father's love.

The needle was doing its slow, easy swing, not really pointing in any particular direction, and that confused her. Was the Spindle gone again? Had Papa left it?

Or had he not even found it? The way he burst into the 'akhelum, spoke to Ahli, made her think he'd found his own way of detecting the Spindle — perhaps he had created his own compass, or maybe one of his dolls was now capable of finding it. Or, for all she knew, her finding it at last, stepping into it, walking down the stairs, had announced its presence and location to everyone in Sand — a Brother had dragged her out of it, after all, so it hadn't been only her who could go inside.

She wished she knew how it worked, what it was and

what it did, aside from just lead to the Leshii. Why it showed up sometimes and not others. Why it affected this old compass as it did.

She could feel Shahif and the queen both watching her, apparently waiting for her to do something, though Ember wasn't sure what they expected to see her do.

As she looked at the compass, the needle started to spin. It had been moving the whole time, but in that lazy, unfocused way it had during the times Ember couldn't find the Spindle from outside the 'akhelum. Now, there was purpose there. Speed and intent. The needle whipped around the face like a revving copter blade, and everything inside Ember's gut shifted toward her feet.

Something was happening. She didn't know what, but the compass needle didn't spin like that over nothing.

She had to get back to the Spindle.

Ember started to push herself up, her first instinct to run for the 'akhelum and find out what was going on and what she was supposed to do about it, but pain raced up her arms — well, her left arm; her right had no feeling left below the queen's knot, but that in itself was almost as bad as the pain — and reminded her of what she should never have forgotten, not even for an instant.

She was useless.

She sagged back down, but her eyes stayed fixed on the compass.

"What's it doing?"

Shahif's attention had shifted to the compass as well, and the frown on his face had turned from sympathy and concern to confusion and worry.

He was a Brother, or at least had been. She'd never had the chance to find out what they knew about the Spindle, about the Leshii — maybe he would be able to tell her. "It's … something's happening."

Shahif's eyes widened and he opened his mouth, but the queen spoke the word first.

"Mikail."

Ember looked up at her. Her lips were pressed together into a single thin line, her dark brow pulled tight down over her even darker eyes. Ember knew that expression — it was the same one the queen had given her time and time again. It was the one that meant the queen was done playing polite and now expected results. She, too, was watching the compass, but the way she said Papa's name made it clear that it wasn't a small metal circle she was seeing, but Mikail Dominikovich's face.

Ember felt that determination — the queen's determination — leak into her own limbs.

Papa was doing something. He'd found the Spindle, and it was her job, her *purpose*, to help him fix the Leshii.

Whatever he thought about her in this state, however he might feel about that fact, that was what he'd promised her. They would fix the Leshii and save the world, together. Everything, every dream, every mystery, every thread of her life she'd ever pulled at, and even the ones she'd never examined before — everything about her had been leading her to this point.

Injured, useless, too weak to stand, it didn't matter.

This was what she was meant to do. Now, she just had to do it.

Chapter Twenty-One

"Help me up."

Ember wasn't speaking to either Shahif or the queen particularly, just to whoever would help her first. But both of the other people in the room stared at her as if she had lost whatever was left of her mind.

Ember set her jaw and breathed until the pain and frustration eased. They hadn't heard her thoughts, didn't understand her purpose — she shouldn't be annoyed at them for not helping her to do something she clearly wasn't ready for.

She looked at Shahif, who was, she supposed, the most likely to be sympathetic to her. "Shahif, please. Something's happening, and the Leshii needs me."

"You're so weak," he protested.

Ember flinched involuntarily. She knew he didn't mean it like that, but the words stung anyway. She kept her voice level, as calm as she could make it. "I know. That's why I need help."

"You need to rest. Get your strength back. Don't worry about Mikail — you can't do anything about it like this."

"Oh, honestly," the queen tutted. "She's not made of glass." She stepped around Shahif, crouched in front of Ember, and looped one arm around Ember's shoulders. Together, with Ember sitting up and the queen holding her steady, Ember was able to pry herself off the floor, and once the black dots receded from the corners of her eyes and she let the queen take some of her weight, she was able to get onto her feet.

Her whole body ached fiercely at the motion, and the effort sent a fresh pulse of blood down both her arms. The bandage around the cut on her left wrist grew damp again, and her right arm tingled with new feeling as a few drops forced their way past the tourniquet only to drip out onto the floor. But the queen was sturdy at Ember's side and didn't waver when Ember slumped for a moment against her shoulder.

And, once that moment was up and the black spots had once again retreated from her vision, she took a step, then another. The queen stepped with her, and if Ember let her take a little more of her weight than she would've cared to admit, the other woman didn't say anything about it.

"Right," she said and glanced back at Shahif, who was watching them with a frown, disapproving but unable to say anything more. "Grab the compass for me, won't you?"

He scooped up the compass, then even stood up and opened the door. "You shouldn't," he whispered as Ember and the queen pushed past him.

Ember almost smiled. The expression came out a bit more twisted and pained than she meant it to, but it came out, and that was about as good as she could hope for. "I have to."

Shahif didn't argue further. Instead, he closed his fingers around the compass the way she would've if she could, stepped out of the room, and closed the door behind them. "Lead on, mustafi."

EMBER DIDN'T ACTUALLY DO MUCH of the leading. After realizing that nothing he could say or do would likely stop her, Shahif took her unspoken request to show them the way and stepped forward to guide them, first through the qasun, then toward the 'akhelum.

Ember kept her eyes mostly either on her feet or the compass. Even in Shahif's hand, the needle kept up its whirling, suggesting to her that whatever it was Papa was doing, it was enough to make Spindle and compass react even not under her own touch.

She wasn't sure how she felt about that idea — the Spindle was supposed to be hers. Hers to find, to enter, to explore. Why had it suddenly gone from being unreachable when Eli was too close, to accessible by someone who wasn't her at all?

She shook that thought out of her head. It was selfish to think she ought to be the only one able to reach the Spindle, the only one able to hold the compass and understand what it was trying to say. She didn't know what drove the Spindle to do anything that it did, and it was her father who was there now.

She wouldn't be selfish or jealous of her own father.

The 'akhelum door hung open by only its bottom hinge, the upper two warped and broken by what could've only been a doll's strength. No one stopped them as they entered.

Ember wasn't exactly one to be worried about the Brothers, but the fact that they weren't guarding the door struck her as a bad sign. And from almost the moment they stepped through the door, Ember could hear noises echoing down the hall, shouts and grunts and something combative that sounded like metal against metal.

Shahif wasn't paying them much attention anymore — he hurried down the hall with confident steps, his pace encouraging Ember and the queen to pick up theirs. His eyes were fixed on something not currently visible, and Ember guessed he was leading them, not toward the Spindle necessarily, but toward the sounds of fighting.

She tugged the queen along, urging her to go a little faster despite the fact that Ember herself was puffing and stumbling already at the speed. But she didn't want to lose Shahif in the twisty darkness of the 'akhelum halls, which they were in real danger of doing.

They followed, and with every step, the noises got louder, closer, until they turned a corner and nearly tripped over a body.

Ember blinked and stumbled to a stop, unprepared to find herself staring at the dead stare of another person. He was a Brother and lay like Ahli had, with his head tilted oddly to one side but no visible wounds.

Shahif crouched down beside him, fingers passing along his neck like he was checking for a heartbeat, but that was pointless — he was already dead.

More bodies like this one littered the hall heading toward the room where the Brothers had taken her and cut off her hand. Ember shivered.

She'd always figured dolls weren't technically as harmless as they'd always appeared. Guessed that, if they wanted to, they could be dangerous. But, though that idea lived somewhere in the back of her mind, she'd never given it much thought, wasn't used to the idea of dolls fighting, dolls killing. Of course it was *possible* — anything with the ability to move could potentially be dangerous — but that didn't mean it was *true*.

Her thoughts flashed to Felix, to the splash of red that had almost caught her attention when she saw Papa and his dolls come into the room. Was he responsible for this carnage?

Surely not. Felix was a doll, but that didn't make him not himself.

Did it?

The fact that she couldn't readily answer that question spooked her. She pushed it aside, reminded herself that wasn't what they were here for.

The Spindle. She had to get to the Spindle, and never mind questions about what dolls were for now. They were dangerous, and apparently willing to prove it, and that was all she needed for now.

"They're dead, Shahif," she said when Shahif moved from the first Brother on the ground to the next. "All of them."

"They're…" His voice faded off, and when he looked up from the Brother at his feet, his eyes were shiny. "I don't understand."

"Dolls," the queen answered before Ember could. "Mikail always insisted that they come programmed with some fight in them."

Ember looked over at her. There was a grim set to her mouth, and she let her eyes skip over the bodies in the hall without paying them any particular attention, like she'd seen this sort of thing before.

Ember had never really wondered much about the queen of Frost — it seemed a pointless exercise, and all she needed to know was obvious enough from the few times they'd spoken. But her expression now, the words that suggested she knew more than she had let on about — well, certainly about dolls and Papa, and who knew what else — maybe she was worth more consideration than Ember had given her before.

But, again, not now.

"We need to go." She didn't need to see the compass to know that. The more they moved through the 'akhelum halls, the closer they got to the sounds, the harder that little sensation deep in Ember's chest pulled at her. Underneath everything else, the surprise of discovering bodies, the flashes of curiosity about the queen, that pull remained consistent.

And it was growing. Pleading. Yanking.

Ember took the lead now, still leaning against the queen for a bit of support to her obnoxiously weak knees, but not needing the guidance of Shahif to find where she needed to go. She stepped carefully around the bodies — she felt no love for the Brothers, no particular grief to see a few of them ended, but they were people even after everything, and she took care not to strike them with her feet or brush them with her hem, just in case that mattered to their souls.

Shahif stood up and followed, whispering to himself, or maybe to the bodies, too low to hear words but with a rhythm to his words that sounded practiced and ritualized. Some kind of last rites, perhaps.

Ember didn't interrupt him.

At the end of the hallway was the room where the Brothers had brought her. This door, too, hung open by twisted hinges, and through it, she could see a couple of Brothers fighting a couple of dolls, and even more broken-necked corpses, including Ahli where he'd fallen. These final Brothers were responsible for the noises echoing down the hallway, but it was clear with only a single look that this wasn't where Papa and most of his dolls had ended up. It wasn't, after all, where the Spindle lived.

Ember moved past the room before she could get a more thorough look of it, before she could accidentally catch sight of, say, her hand on the floor or recognize any faces besides Ahli's amongst the bodies.

Eli hadn't been in this room before. She knew that for certain, even though she didn't see everyone in there during her capture. Wherever Eli was, he couldn't be one of the corpses on the floor, because he wasn't one of the Brothers in the room before.

Wherever he was, he was fine. He was cleverer than any of the Brothers — he would know not to engage with a doll. He would've hidden somewhere away from this rampaging army, or he would've offered Papa help, joined the army before they hurt him.

He was a Dusk boy at heart. A survivor. And he would've recognized the prince of Sand, either because Ember had told him who he was, or by just recognizing his face. Eli was fine.

He had to be.

The noises grew quiet again as they passed the room, Ember allowing herself to be pulled forward by instinct, by the thread of awareness that connected her to the Spindle.

They turned the corner, and there, in the wall like the stones had been torn open from the inside, was the Spindle.

Chapter Twenty-Two

SHAHIF, and even the queen, paused at the sight, their footsteps hesitating and their jaws loosening with surprise and awe.

Ember grinned. "That's what I thought."

Shahif recovered first, enough for words at least. "It's ... real."

That was not the reaction Ember would've guessed from him. He was a Brother, or had been at some point — surely, he'd known the Spindle was real. But his tone was amazed, slightly disbelieving, as if Atalanta herself had descended from the heavens to announce that, whatever the skeptics might say, praying to her worked every time.

But even as they paused there to admire the fact of it, something was wrong. Ember couldn't quite decide at first what it was, why a strange sense of wrongness tickled her insides as she pried herself away from the queen and took a couple of experimental steps forward on her own. Her legs still felt a little wobbly, her consciousness mildly uncertain, but the walk through the qasun and 'akhelum had reminded her body how to move, how to walk, and her legs obeyed her completely under her own power.

But that wasn't the wrongness she was feeling. That was just the pain and blood loss, and those sensations were becoming familiar now. This was something else, something deeper, a slimy sense of wrongness that touched her in the same place as the Leshii did.

She reached the Spindle, took that step through the stones and into the top room, and that wrongness crashed through her. It filled her like the little pool of slime deep inside her had suddenly cracked its barriers and flooded her everywhere. Her stomach lurched, and for a moment, she had to clench her teeth and swallow against the urge to be sick.

This room had shined with sunlight and gold when she first saw it; now, even though light still poured through the windows, it was coming through dirty panes. The gold of the room had rusted to a sort of bronze, and the whole place smelled faintly of used oil.

Ember hurried for the steps in the center of the room. Dimly, she could hear Shahif and the queen following her, their footsteps scrambling down the tight spiral stairs after her.

Every room of the stairs was similarly wrong. She hadn't gotten a great look at every one the first time, but she did remember them being each as bright and fascinating as the top room was. Now, the one with the plants was no longer blooming, and the room of gears and machines seemed to be in a bit more disarray than before. By the time she reached the bottom of the stairs, Ember was almost running, and she hit the final floor at a speed that made her trip and fall on her still-iffy legs.

She reached out automatically to break her fall with her hands, and fresh, brilliant pain raced through her arms as her wounds took the brunt of her weight. Ember bit down on a scream, but some of it still escaped her throat. Fresh blood oozed from the wounds, smearing across the ground when she rolled over. Tears poked her eyes and slid through her squeezed-shut lids.

"Ember?"

Shahif was there, crouching at her side, his voice worried.

"I'm okay," Ember lied. "Tripped."

"Take a deep breath."

She obeyed, forcing air through her teeth and down into her lungs. It came out of her tripping over a sob; she turned the sound into a cough instead.

The fresh agony faded, settling back into the pervasive but much duller ache she was starting to get used to, and she sat up again. "Rotting Brothers," she spat, because it felt good to let out some of that pain as anger — at least anger didn't feel quite so helpless, even when it didn't do anything.

The queen nudged Ember's leg with her toe. "C'mon. Up you get."

"Give her a minute!" Shahif hissed.

"We don't have a minute," the queen answered and tilted her head in the direction of the Leshii.

Ember followed her eyes, and all thoughts of pain and the Brothers vanished as quickly as they had come.

Because there was Papa, standing at the base of the Leshii and pulling at some of the rusty panels that covered up the innards of the engine. Beside him, smashed together into too little space, were many of his dolls, but not dolls the way Ember had ever seen them.

She was used to dolls being like people, shaped close enough to humans that, if she didn't know what to look for, she could actually mistake them for people. She *had* mistaken one for a person, even after knowing what dolls were and how to identify them.

These dolls weren't even dolls anymore, those people-shaped mechanical beings she was familiar with. They were parts of dolls. Limbs and heads rearranged and mashed together into new shapes, bits of them wired into different bits of other dolls so the whole thing was a mass of eyes and fingers and legs that didn't connect the way they should. The whole thing crackled with electricity.

A flash of red caught Ember's eye as it always did, as it always would no matter how she tried to pretend otherwise, and she couldn't stop herself from seeing.

Felix was in that mess, though only his head and one hand were visible from where she sat.

Ember got to her feet. Her stomach roiled, but she choked the sensation down. She wasn't seeing Papa or the other dolls, or even the Leshii, anymore — her eyes were fixed on Felix, on the horror of not knowing what had happened to him.

A hand snagged the back of her tunic and tugged her to the side. At the same time, another hand slid across her mouth to hold in the scream building in her throat, as if the person grabbing her knew that she would scream at the touch.

She started to turn, to kick Shahif where it would hurt for grabbing her like that, but the person held her a little tighter and whispered low in her ear. "Shh. Ember, it's me."

"Eli!" she gasped, though the sound was muffled by his hand.

"Shh!" he hissed again, and she noticed now that he was standing behind a tree, peering around as if hiding from Papa and the dolls.

She nodded once, and he lowered his hand from her

mouth, though his other one stayed tight on the back of her tunic as if worried that she might wander away from him if he let go.

"What're you doing here?" she whispered.

He didn't answer. His gaze kept straying back toward Felix, too, his brow creasing with confusion.

"Dolls. All of them," she said.

"All?"

Had Ember not told him? Everything of the last several days had gotten jumbled and confused inside her thoughts, and now she couldn't quite remember what she had and had not done.

But now wasn't the time to go into detail. Maybe she'd never feel right about it. For the sake of brevity, she just nodded and went back to watching Papa, trying to figure out what, exactly, he was up to and why every touch of his fingers against the Leshii felt like he was ruffling that oily feeling of wrongness inside her.

He'd finished peeling away the outer panel he had his hands against and moved on to the one beside it. Ember watched, carefully, letting her attention snag on what it would.

The inner workings of the Leshii were just as perfect as she'd dreamed they were. The more of the rusty outer panels Papa removed, the better she could see them, the gears and belts and pistons that connected with such precision they couldn't have been the result of fallible human hands. Their stillness made her sad — a machine that beautiful shouldn't be allowed to go still and rust away.

What was Papa looking for?

And what was he doing with a mass of half-disassembled dolls?

He pried off another outer panel, and Ember winced

as she realized why just that motion made her feel wrong. He was *skinning* the Leshii.

She almost leaped away from the tree at that, gave up her advantage to run over to Papa and beg him to stop. This wasn't the way to do it — she didn't need to know the right way to turn the Engine back on to know that this wasn't it.

The right way didn't involve tearing chunks off the engine. He didn't need to mangle it to figure out what was broken and fix it.

She swallowed down her horror. It was just a machine, and sometimes to fix what was broken inside a machine, a person had to open it up, expose its innermost workings.

Except … the Leshii wasn't *just* a machine. It wasn't *just* anything.

And Papa was hurting it.

"Ha!" he crowed, the noise cutting suddenly through the unnatural stillness of the trees. He reached inside the Leshii for a moment, and when he pulled his arm back, he was holding a handful of wires.

The pain from Ahli's blade was nothing compared to the strange agony that cut through Ember's gut. It wasn't a physical sensation at all, not like a knife to the ribs or the hollowness of an empty belly, but not completely unlike either of those feelings, either.

Ember gasped, and it all fell into place in that moment. What Papa was doing. What he was about to do. Why he'd reached into the Leshii and ripped out a chunk of its guts.

He was attaching it to an external power source. She'd made that very suggestion herself for his cooling machine after that first dinner.

But she didn't know at the time he would take it to mean it was something he should do on the Leshii.

"No!"

This time, neither her own clenched jaw nor Eli's hand was fast enough to stop the word from coming out of her.

This time, she couldn't keep quiet and just watch.

This time, Papa did hear her. He whirled around, the mess of wires still in his hand.

Ember yanked herself away from Eli's grip and stepped out of the shelter of the tree, ignoring him as he hissed at her to come back and scrabbled to get another hold on her. "Papa, don't."

He scowled at her, his lip curling back in unmistakable disgust. "What are you doing here?"

"It won't work."

"It was your suggestion."

"It's not just any machine, Papa. It's the Leshii. You can't just plug it into a makeshift battery."

"Pff. I'll do as I want."

When had his eyes gotten so manic, his voice so unhinged?

Maybe he'd always been like that, and Ember just refused to notice until now.

He turned to the mass of dolls now, his grotesque battery. "Sand answers to me," he said, low enough that Ember wondered if he was even talking to her anymore. "And now all of Steppe will, too."

He stuck the Leshii's wires against an exposed panel on one doll's head, and, with a single flick of his wrist, snapped the whole thing on.

The doll battery vibrated, and with a terrible scrape and whine of unused metal, something inside the Leshii stirred.

Chapter Twenty-Three

EMBER COULDN'T MOVE. She tried to pry her feet from the spot where she stood, but her legs wouldn't respond to her order. They stayed stuck three steps back from the doll battery and Papa, who watched that vibrating electricity for a long moment, then threw his head back and laughed.

Ember had never heard him — never heard *anyone* — laugh like that. It was too loud even over the crackling of the dolls and the painful grinding from inside the Leshii. Manic and unhinged and terrible.

"Papa—" she tried, but he spun to her, his eyes still glowing, and swatted her with the back of one hand.

Ember stumbled back a step. The strike hadn't hurt, exactly, certainly not enough to cut through all the other pain she was feeling, but the fact that it was Papa's hand, that he'd dismiss her like that, like she was an annoyance he wanted rid of as quickly as possible, still had the power to knock her back.

At least it reminded her legs what movement felt like.

The ground shuddered beneath her feet. A roar was building up inside the Leshii as it was forced to knock rust off its gears, forced to work without even being fixed. Ember felt it growing, as big and terrible as the Great Death itself.

She stumbled back another step and collided with the trunk of a nearby tree. The sickly leaves still clinging to its branches curled at the edges like the tree was bracing itself for what came next.

It wasn't silent — bits of the dolls rattled against one another, and the Leshii made a couple of ear-splitting shrieks as parts that hadn't moved in three generations fought against the compulsion of the battery — but it was all drowned out by that building roar that wasn't even a sound yet, only a sensation.

She had to get out of here. She had to get Eli and Shahif and the queen out of here before the roar broke and killed them all. Papa — her heart wrenched with the realization, but she couldn't pretend it wasn't true — wouldn't be taken away.

Her attention snagged on Felix again, or at least the mangled bits of him she could see. His head and one hand, and maybe that leg there was his.

He didn't deserve this. Of everyone about to be destroyed, he deserved his fate perhaps the least.

She couldn't leave him here, either. Not like this. Not Felix, curious and kind, who loved art and architecture and wanted to see the world beyond Frost's walls.

Papa had turned back to face the Leshii, still laughing that maniac laugh. If she slipped in, nabbed Felix, and slipped back again fast enough, he wouldn't even have a chance to notice a difference.

She started forward, lifting her hands in preparation to unplug Felix from the doll battery — two wires connected his head to the next doll's, and one each to his hand and leg, easy enough to unplug and reconnect to the parts beside them — but the tingling ache from her arms stopped her. Reminded her of what it seemed impossible to forget, that she had yet somehow managed to forget.

She didn't have hands. Even her left one, though still attached to her body, wasn't working.

She was useless. Useless to stop Papa from skinning and gutting the Leshii, and now useless to stop him from using her friend to do it.

But before she could sink to her knees in despair, a hand touched her elbow, and Shahif's voice spoke low into her ear. "What do you need?"

Ember turned. Shahif, Eli, and even the queen stood next to her, all watching her, waiting for directions on what to do next.

"Felix," she answered. It wasn't enough, but it was all she could manage through a tight throat and the threat of tears.

And Shahif — Atalanta bless him! — understood. He followed Ember's gaze to Felix, then glanced first at Papa, then at Eli. "You," he said with his eyes on Eli, summoning. "With me."

Another glance, at the queen this time. "Get her out of here. We'll be right behind with the doll."

She shouldn't go. She couldn't. The Leshii was hurt, and Papa wasn't fixing it, and the whole world had gone suddenly all wrong all at once.

But the queen's arm was back at Ember's shoulders, and Ember didn't have the physical strength in her to resist that silent but ice-hard pull. She stumbled, but the queen only held her tighter as they hurried toward the Spindle stairs.

But the stairs were gone. Vanished from the place they'd just been — all that remained were the twisted, dying trees of the Leshii's twisted, dying forest.

The queen hissed under her breath noises that were probably words but mostly just came out as air. After a couple of such noises, she spoke, still low and hissy. "Which way are we facing?"

Ember couldn't tell. The ground beneath her feet trembled. The trees trembled. Her whole body shook.

"Forget it. This way."

As if she had any other option beneath the queen's arm.

They ran, at least as best they could without Ember actually losing her footing. Ember tried to look back, but she couldn't turn her shoulders enough to see Papa or the dolls when she tried.

All she could hear, with her ears and her mind, was the roar of the Leshii.

Ember's story continues...

Lady of Dawn, Book 3 of *The Frost Trilogy* takes Ember and Eli beyond Sand and Frost to a new land. After losing so much, can they keep fighting?

Get Lady of Dawn today!

A Note From The Author

If you enjoyed this book, please take a moment to write a short review on your favorite online bookstore so other readers can enjoy it, too.

Thanks so much!
Aria Noble

About the Author

Aria Noble tells stories of ordinary girls thrust into extraordinary worlds full of mysteries and magic. Her characters aren't afraid to question their assumptions, discover their strength, and possibly even change the world along the way. Fans of Shannon Hale, Phillip Pullman, and Marissa Meyer will love Aria Noble.

Also By Aria Noble

The Frost Trilogy

Queen of Frost

The Prince of Sand

Lady of Dawn

Stand-Alone Novels

Alien Fairytales: The Complete Collection